F
KILLEEN
Kevin
NORTHWEST BRANCH
Try to kiss a girl
30051000232345

# Try to Kiss a Girl

JEFFERSON COUNTY LIBRARY
NORTHWEST BRANCH
5680 STATE RD. PP
HIGH RIDGE, MO 63049

Kevin Killeen

NO LONGER PROPERTY OF
JEFFERSON COUNTY LIBRARY

Blank Slate Press | Saint Louis, Missouri

JEFFERSON COUNTY LIBRARY
NORTHWEST BRANCH

**Blank Slate Press**

adventures in publishing
www.blankslatepress.com

[ Blank Slate Press was founded in 2010 to discover, nurture, publish, and promote new voices from the greater Saint Louis region and beyond. ]

Copyright © 2014 Kevin Killeen
All rights reserved.

Published in the United States by Blank Slate Press, Saint Louis, Missouri 63110. No part of this book may be reproduced, scanned, or distributed in any printed or electronic form without written permission from the publisher, Blank Slate Press, LLC. Please do not participate in or encourage piracy of copyrighted materials in violation of the author's rights.

This is a work of fiction. Any resemblance to actual events or locales or persons, living or dead, is merely coincidental, and names, characters, places, and incidents are either the products of the author's imagination or are used fictitiously.

Cover design Kristina Blank Makansi
Interior design by Kristina Blank Makansi
Cover photo courtesy of Jay Webber

Library of Congress Control Number: 2014941245
ISBN: 978-0-9858086-0-0

PRINTED IN THE UNITED STATES OF AMERICA

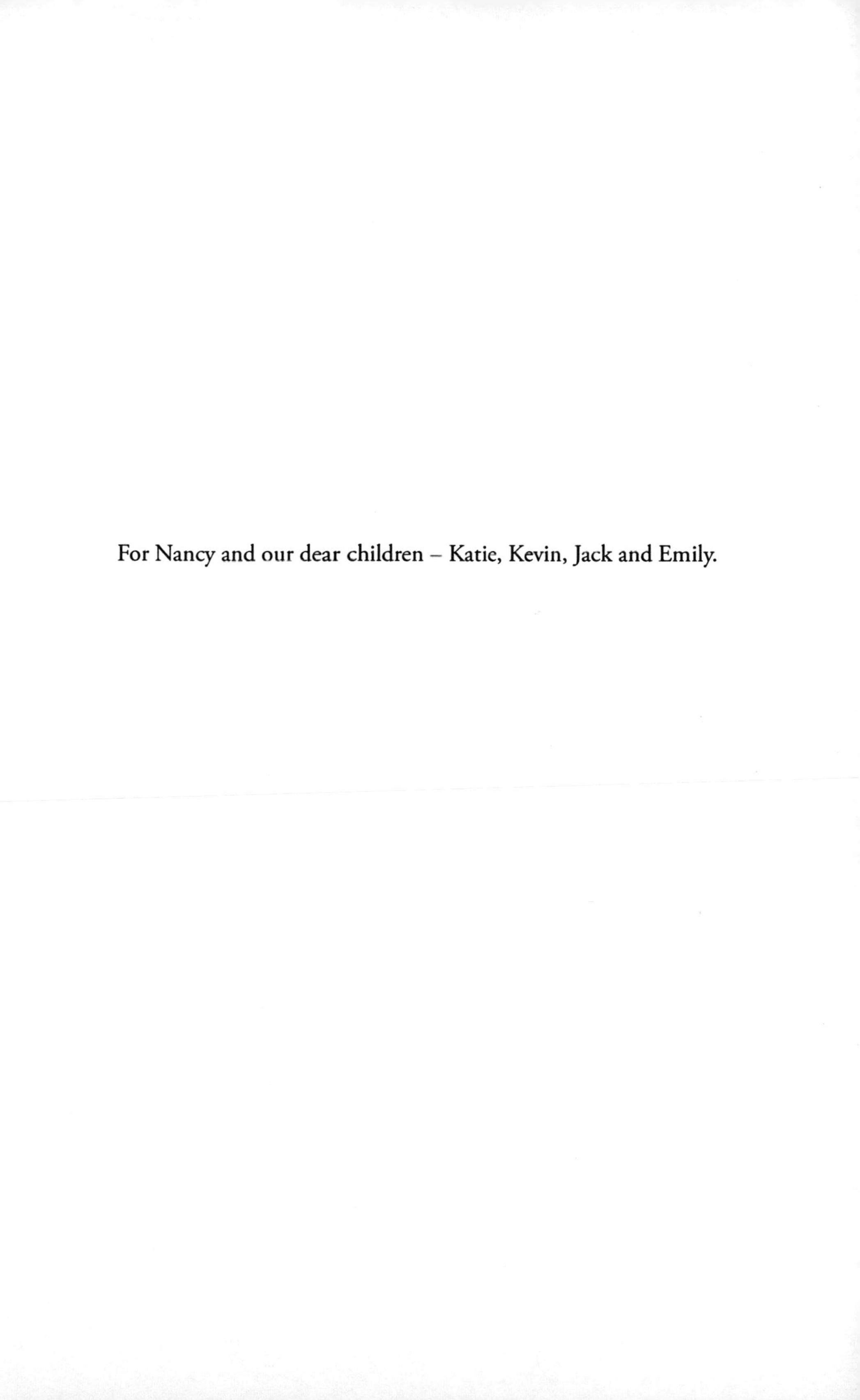

For Nancy and our dear children – Katie, Kevin, Jack and Emily.

# Try to Kiss a Girl

# - chapter one -

THE FAMILY STATION WAGON with luggage piled on top soared up Interstate 57 through an infinity of Illinois corn. Dad, Mom, and all five kids were bound for a week of summer vacation in the lusty resort town of Grand Haven, Michigan. With pistons cranking, oil and antifreeze suffering, and new tires humming, the Buick sliced through wavy mirages of heat rising off the pavement. Passing trucks growled. Farm smells made the boys yell, "Gross!" This was the desperately hot middle of the ride, and the whole Cantwell family was wilting.

"Can we *please* turn on the air conditioner?" Mom mumbled again, feeling every bit of eight months pregnant.

"Oh, I'd love to. Believe me," Dad said, "but in *this* heat? I don't want to break down and have my family stranded in the middle of—"

"I know, I know," Mom moaned, closing her eyes to try to nap. But every few seconds the tires went over a pavement seam with a *thump, thump* while the baby kicked her ribs along with the rhythm. Dad tapped at the temperature gauge as if he could keep the engine cool from the driver's seat. Baking in the middle seat, the younger kids—Teddy, Elizabeth, and baby Joey—endured the heat with blinking eyes and faces pink from the oven breeze blasting through the open windows. Every window in the car was open, even the way back window where the two oldest kids, John and Patrick, sat facing backwards.

"How about this?" Patrick said, holding up an empty Wonder Bread bag. It had been a long time since they'd stopped to go to the bathroom. Now with his bladder full from sneaking an extra orange soda from the cooler, Patrick held the Wonder Bread bag open and looked out the rear window like a tail gunner on a B-24 watching the landscape speed away in reverse.

"Sure, why not," John said.

Patrick got on his knees and unzipped, while John checked the bag for holes. John was the cool, older brother—just a year older—but he knew how to maintain a confident, John Lennon expression during a crisis. Patrick spied up front to see if anyone was watching. Mom was half asleep with her red hair blowing in the wind. Dad chewed on a businessman's breath mint, jaw muscles clenching and unclenching, while his eyes squinted back and forth from the road to the temperature gauge. He was always chewing those breath mints because a dad with a downtown executive job was under a lot of stress. In the middle seat, Teddy, Elizabeth, and baby Joey sat looking forward and didn't know anything.

"I don't see any holes," John said, "but if it springs a leak, stop going."

Patrick opened fire into the Wonder Bread bag. It was a breezy, good, sneaky feeling to pee inside a moving car, like filling up a water balloon to throw at a teacher at the school picnic. Patrick zipped up and took his turn holding the bag so John could go. John was a good aim and didn't get any on Patrick's hands. The more he peed, the heavier the bag got.

"Just don't drop it in the car," John whispered.

John was half finished when Elizabeth reared her head over the seat back, like Godzilla peeking over a row of burning buildings. She was only three, but she could blow flames and destroy the boys with a single word to Mom or Dad. She leaned over boxes of Pampers stuffed between the middle and the way back seat. John wanted to stop peeing but couldn't. No boy could. They could have had a game show on TV called *Try to Stop Peeing for a Thousand Dollars,* and no boy would ever win. Patrick felt that fast-heart-beat fear like in the principal's office. He was sure Elizabeth would scream and Dad would slam on the brakes, the car would screech to a halt, and Mom would yell at them while the bag of pee sloshed everywhere. But Elizabeth was so little she didn't know anything was wrong. She thought seeing boys peeing into Wonder Bread bags was just part of the color and movement and birdsong of life.

"Sit back down, Elizabeth," John whispered, smiling.

She smiled and slid back down in the middle seat looking forward.

"We better hurry up," Patrick whispered.

John and Patrick peeked up front again. With Mom asleep, Dad was looking to the side at a faded, falling-apart barn. The boys might have been making a hydrogen bomb in the way back seat and he wouldn't know. Dad looked at the barn and wondered who died and what happened to their family. Did they stick together? Or scatter? Dad was imagining the farmer's family, years ago, all together saying grace, having dinner and drinking milk during the Great Depression. It's a sad reminder, Dad thought, rubbing his neck. The old barn didn't remind Patrick of anything, but working downtown made dads worry about everything.

"All clear," John whispered.

Patrick closed the top of the Wonder Bread bag and spun it around tight. Together, they lifted it out the back window and let it go.

*SGPESHHHHHHH!* Their bomb hit the hot pavement and exploded. Millions of pee drops bounced and sparkled on the highway like a galaxy expanding on public television. The boys couldn't believe it. A huge, golden vapor cloud rose up and shrouded the road behind them—obscuring everything except for a black speck in the distance.

"Uh-oh," John said. "Bikers!"

The motorcycle gang, clad in black leather and fringe, raced toward the vapor cloud, their chrome wheels spinning in the sun.

"Duck!" Patrick said as he dove below the window with John right beside him. They stared at each other, eyes wide, and listened as the motorcycle engines roared. Dad looked in the rearview mirror and called out, "We need gas. Anyone feel like stopping?"

"No!" John and Patrick yelled together as the middle seat kids whined for a stop. Daring a peek out the back window, John and Patrick saw the gang in sunglasses and red bandanas blaze into the sparkling urine mist. The empty Wonder Bread bag whipped off the tire of the lead bike and stuck on the hot tailpipe of another motorcycle. The boys ducked back down behind a row of sand buckets and beach towels.

"*Shit,* they could be Hell's Angels," John whispered.

"Hell's what?"

"*Hell's Angels!* Don't you know *any*thing?"

"Is that bad?"

"They'll probably kill us."

Patrick pulled his zipper up all the way to hide any evidence of recent urination. John tugged at the bangs of his Beatle haircut. "They'll probably beat Dad to death with chains," he whispered, "then kidnap the rest of us and kill us later."

The station wagon approached an exit ramp, and Dad flipped on the Buick's turn signal. BLINK-BLOCK, BLINK-BLOCK, BLINK-BLOCK. Patrick turned around to see where they were going. Rising above the trees, a SHELL sign came into view. But something was wrong—the "S" was missing.

"Hell," Patrick said reading the sign aloud.

They were going to HELL.

"Oh, God." He ducked back down and squeezed his eyes shut. "Please let them keep going, please, please, please," he prayed in his mind, "and I promise I won't do anything bad the whole trip."

The gang was right behind them as the station wagon slowed to take the exit ramp.

Patrick listened. He knew if the motorcycle engines grew fainter, it meant they were safe. But if they got louder, the whole family would get killed.

The engines got louder—and louder and louder.

A dread like death row before midnight descended on the way back seat. All appeals were exhausted. The boys couldn't stand it. They looked up to face their doom and saw a miracle. Apparently, the bikers didn't realize what had happened. The gang was staying on the highway, as the station wagon veered off. Patrick watched the lead biker, a Viking-like fat man with a red beard. Sitting behind him, with her arms wrapped around his waist, was a woman in a halter-top. Her long braid whipped in the wind as the motorcycles shot under a bridge, and the Buick rose off the interstate like a B-24 lifting through the clouds after a bombing run. The family was safe.

"I'm proud of you all for holding it so long," Dad called out. "Time to tinkle."

# - chapter two -

PATRICK FORGOT all about his prayer as he and John jumped out the back window. Forgetting a prayer was probably a sin, but an answered prayer always seemed like nothing more than luck when the trouble was past, especially on vacation. God was in heaven thinking of nuns and floods and planetary orbits, not bikers and Wonder Bread bags. He looked up at the Shell station sign—HELL. Beneath the sign lay a graveyard of rusty and forsaken junk cars, cars that other families had once packed up for their own vacations. The sun poured out its fury on the asphalt, smacking everyone in the face with a pungent blend of gasoline, oil drippings, and far-away cow manure. Dad got out and checked the ropes holding the luggage on top of the car. His Battleship Missouri knots—he had been a sailor during the war—were as tight as guitar strings. Patrick watched him in his green plaid short-sleeved shirt and short pants with white socks and Converse tennis shoes as he walked around the car checking the tires and closely inspecting the wood grain decal for any scratches the kids might have made recently.

"Help you folks?" A man in a blue uniform shirt with gray hair jogged out to fill up the car. His nametag said "Al," and he had a quick smile and dark sweat stains under his armpits. He had been working in the mechanic's bay on a brake job when the station wagon rolled over the pink hose ringing the bell for service. This was his own station, which he bought a few years back after working years as a mechanic for other bosses. Now he was the boss, but he was working harder than ever and couldn't take a summer vacation. It was the money-making season, and the caravans of vacation families fleeing the heat heading north, had to be served.

"Yes, sir, I'm worried about my antifreeze," Dad said, popping the hood. Al wiped his hands on his blue pants and took a look. On the other side of the car, in her capri pants, loafers, and maternity blouse, Mom stretched her back and scratched her belly before opening the back door to check Joey's diaper. That was the grossest part about being a mom—being in charge of the poo. Patrick looked around for something exciting to do and hurried away from the car so he wouldn't catch a whiff, just in case. Off to the side of the building, he spied a little tent marked "FIREWORKS!"

Mom glanced up, saw him eyeing the tent, and shouted, "Hey Patrick, no fireworks!" before he could even start that direction.

"Aw." He kicked a bottle cap on the asphalt in disgust.

"And Patrick," Dad added, "I want you and John to stick together with Teddy and look both ways."

The three boys walked into the office. A wood shim with cruddy footprints from the mechanics' shoes propped open the front door. There was no air conditioning, only a box fan blowing hot air and a Shell No Pest Strip twirling overhead. Behind the counter a seventeen-year-old with long hair and a "Dave" nametag on his blue shirt listened to "Let the Sunshine In" on the radio, bobbing his chin to the beat, surrounded by shelves of STP cans, fan belts, beef jerky, and chewing gum.

"Folks need some fireworks?" Dave asked.

"No, thank you. May we please use your restrooms?" Mom said, walking in behind the boys, holding baby Joey in one arm and nudging Elizabeth along with her free hand.

"On the right."

Mom took Joey and Elizabeth into the ladies' room while John took Teddy into the men's room. Patrick hovered by the magazine rack and reached for an *Archie* comic book, whistling to the song on the radio. He had never noticed "Let the Sunshine In" before, but it was as thick as steam on him now. Just then, the black rotary phone on the counter rang loud and jangly, and Dave picked it up. It was his girlfriend, the one he'd taken to the Land of Lincoln Drive-In the other night to see *Romeo and Juliet*.

"Hey, baby." Dave's voice changed, and he started talking all smooth and low as he twiddled the cord and looked longingly through the haze out toward the highway.

Patrick read half a page of *Archie*. He felt a mild interest in Veronica, but he was getting bored with Archie and his friends. So he ditched that and picked up a fishing magazine. An article on northern pike warned they have teeth that can cut you to ribbons if you're not careful.

"Well, maybe we should get together *again*," Dave whispered.

"Let the Sun Shine In" seemed to take over the room. Patrick didn't know what the words meant, but he was all for it—whatever it was. The women singing had such beautiful, understanding voices. He tapped his foot to the beat and put down the fishing magazine. Then he slipped a different magazine out of the rack and opened it to a color photo of three women getting out of a car at a picnic site by a lake. Patrick always liked picnics, so he turned the page. Now the women were wading into the lake—naked.

What?

Patrick slapped it shut and looked around for Dad. He was standing outside by the car with the hood up and steam rising from the engine while Al poured green liquid in the radiator. Mom was still in the bathroom, and, behind the counter, Dave talked on the phone, twirled the cord, and stared out the window. Patrick opened the magazine back up to see what this was all about.

He hadn't been mistaken. The women were wading into a perfectly calm lake perfectly and completely naked. Their round bottoms were showing, whiter than the rest of their skin, and one of them was turned so he could see she had breasts as free as the bosoms on the statues at the St. Louis Art Museum, the ones Dad always led the boys past quickly on the way to the basement to see the dead mummy with the black toe. Unlike the breasts at the museum, these weren't green, and they obviously weren't marble. They were alive. Patrick studied them closely as electricity flowed from the magazine page through his eyes into the visual cortex of his brain, nearly making his hair stand on end. The women on the radio kept singing "Let the Sunshine In" as if the song were just for him, him and those naked women on the picnic, and he just stood there looking and looking and looking.

Suddenly, the ladies' room door swung open, and Mom walked out carrying Joey and leading Elizabeth by the hand. "You're too young for gum," she told Elizabeth. "You might swallow it and choke."

"I won't."

Like lightning, Patrick shoved the magazine back into the rack—upside down and crooked—and grabbed the Archie comic and opened it.

"You already go to the bathroom?" Mom asked.

"Oh, yeah … I went earlier."

"Well, let's go."

"But I'm looking at magazines."

She zoomed in on the *Archie* comic book in his hand with eyes that had her checking-for-poo look. She scanned the magazine rack in front of him, reading the titles, and then hitched up Joey a bit on her hip and studied Patrick's face. Before he could stop himself, he swallowed, and his eyes darted over to the magazine with the naked women. It was crooked and out of line. Mom followed his glance and noticed it, too. Her face darkened, and she took a step forward. Patrick stopped breathing and tried to concentrate back on the comic book where Jughead was doing something stupid, but all he could see was that Betty and Veronica also had breasts like the women on the picnic, and he wondered vaguely why he had never noticed them before.

Just then, Dad walked in to pay for the gas, and Elizabeth yelled, "DADDY, CAN I HAVE GUM?"

"Why, sure." He smiled and patted her shoulder.

Mom whirled around. "Wait, she always swallows it."

Joey started crying.

While no one was looking, Patrick put down the *Archie* comic, grabbed the naked-woman magazine, and whipped it behind the display rack where it ruffled to the floor and stayed until 1985 when Al retired and a work crew halted demolition of the gas station to flip through its pages, admiring the women's breasts and round white bottoms. With Mom and Dad buying Elizabeth gum, Patrick hurried out to the car.

"Everybody feeling better now?" Dad asked.

As the car pulled away, Patrick took a deep breath. He was confused. John was next to him in their regular spot in the way back seat. He wanted to tell John what he'd seen and ask him what it meant. But John had his nose in the July issue of *Beatles Book* magazine, which he brought from St. Louis along with his other Beatles reading material. John knew a lot about life and was old enough to cut other people's lawns without chopping his foot off. He was supposed to be saving money for the future, but mostly he spent it on guitar strings, picks, and sketchpads to practice drawing. A few weeks back, John had drawn a picture of movie star Raquel Welch. It was after Dad let the boys stay up late to learn about history and watch Welch in the movie *One Million Years B.C.* John's drawing showed her shapely figure in a skimpy bearskin outfit, and Dad stuck it up on the refrigerator, praising it and saying it showed John had talent. When Mom saw it the next morning, she moaned and rolled her eyes at Dad. She said John should have drawn the dinosaurs, *not the cave woman.*

"John, you gonna do any artwork this trip?" Patrick was warming him up to ask him about the magazine.

"I guess."

"You bring your sketch pad?"

"Yeah, why?"

Patrick hesitated. He figured John must know *something* about why those women were at a picnic with no clothes on, but he was afraid to ask because on a recent family trip to see Abraham Lincoln's home in Springfield and learn about Civil War history, he had asked John about those machines in the men's room at gas stations, the ones that truckers put quarters into and turned the knobs, and John had told him to "ask Mom and Dad." That was a sure tip-off that something was up, because that's what Mom and Dad had told both John and Patrick to say to Teddy if he ever asked about something he wasn't supposed to know about, like why the notes Santa left on the mantel looked like Mom's handwriting.

Curiosity won out, though, and Patrick had asked Dad about the machines and the truck drivers. Dad sighed and got all sad like whenever he saw a collapsed barn. He told Patrick not to look at those machines anymore. That was it. That's all he said. He never gave him any good information about them. Those machines were some kind of secret more important than the entire Lincoln industry. Patrick knew Lincoln had done some good, but Lincoln was boring and dead, and truckers were putting quarters in those machines like crazy and getting something secret out of them. And now, here was a magazine with something even more vital and mysterious. John would probably tell him to "just ask Mom and Dad" about it. He couldn't do that. Why miss going to the beach or exploring the woods when they got to the cottage so Dad could sit him down for some long talk while he chewed a breath mint and heaved heavy, sad sighs?

For miles and miles on the highway, all he could think about were those women and how different they were from ones back in St. Louis pushing carts through the grocery store aisles. He knew right away it was bad to see them without clothes on. Nudity was a sin. That's what Mom said the time the babysitter reported the boys had run around with nothing but dishtowels on, pretending they were Charlton Heston in *Planet of the Apes*. Mom told them up and down how nudity was a sin that time. But if it's in a magazine, Patrick thought, this must be some new development in society. Something was going on. Nudity was out there.

Patrick wished this type of breakthrough were covered on the news. One time he'd tried to watch the news straight through, but the only thing anyone talked about was President Nixon, Vietnam, and commercials for Bayer Aspirin. Oh, and the astronauts getting ready to go to the moon. Nothing any good. Patrick tried to forget about the whole thing, but all he could think about was that calm lake and those round white bottoms. Eventually his eyes grew tired as he watched the state of Illinois fade away behind him, and he fell asleep.

# - chapter three -

"DO YOU KNOW where babies come from?" Rex said, flipping a card on the bed. Dressed in his *Mission: Impossible* pajamas, Patrick cautiously put down a card as the thunderstorm drummed in from the lake, lashing and flashing the woods around the red cottage where he was spending the night with his new friend. It was Sunday night. Rex sat across the bed from Patrick, wearing only Fruit of the Loom white underpants.

"Do you know?" Rex repeated, chewing on a spent fudgesicle stick while he tossed down another card. Patrick studied his cards intently. From the bedside table, a plaster Indian chief lamp with a crooked shade cast a yellow light over the game. Damp lake air from the open window blew the curtains and flapped the back page of a *Mad* magazine that Rex had folded earlier to show Patrick the secret pattern hidden in a cartoon. Patrick never could guess beforehand what was hidden on the back of a *Mad* magazine, but it was always there every month just waiting to be discovered.

Rex flipped down another card, bullet fast. *"Well, do you know?"*

"Gimmie a minute. I'm thinking."

Rex looked at Patrick like he was stupid, stupid, stupid. They were both eleven, but Rex seemed to know a lot more than Patrick. He had already shown Patrick all sorts of new things. Getting ready for bed, Rex had pulled out the suitcase under his bed and showed Patrick his paperback copy of *Flying Saucers, Serious Business* with real pictures of spaceships. It was a musty smelling paperback, so apparently people had known about the invasion for a while. But

Patrick hadn't. He'd always thought flying saucers were made up. Rex told him it was a hidden truth President Nixon didn't want people to know about. "When you look at Nixon's face," Rex said, "you can tell he's hiding something." Some of the saucers may have underwater bases in Lake Michigan, Rex explained, which was why he had brought along a pair of binoculars to keep on his bed stand in case they shoot out of the lake at night.

Rex also had an old *Look* magazine he'd swiped from the library. He'd opened it to a dog-eared page with an article about a couple kidnapped by aliens on a dark road in New Hampshire—Betty and Barney Hill. Why hadn't the nuns covered this in science class? Apparently you could be snatched into a spaceship at any time, but mostly at night. Also stuffed in among his pile of secrets, Rex had a newspaper article on Mothman. He was the worst. Mothman was about seven feet tall with wings, and his eyes glowed red at night like bicycle reflectors if anyone pointed a flashlight at him. Rex said some people in West Virginia had seen Mothman a few times in the woods, and next thing they knew a bridge fell into a river and forty-six people got killed.

Rex knew so many mysterious things, and the cottage bedroom was so shadowy that Patrick had tried to change the subject. "Hey, Rex," he said with his voice cracking, "why don't we play cards?" Rex noticed the crack in Patrick's voice, so when he got off the bed to get some cards, he told Patrick *even more* about Mothman. In a prowling whisper he said, "I hear he can fly anywhere he wants, not just West Virginia." Rex added that sometimes he hears strange sounds in the woods behind the cottage and that the path from their back door leads to an old cemetery. Then he stopped short with the cards in his hands and listened toward the open window. "*What's that?* Did you hear something?" There was nothing. Only the sound of the storm building up across the water. Rex was testing Patrick to see if he would try to quit the sleepover, maybe fake a sour stomach and ask to go back to his mommy and daddy. That's one thing Patrick didn't like about Rex. He knew Patrick was scared of the Mothman but kept at it anyway. And now, during the card game, Rex kept asking about babies.

Patrick pretended not to care. He just wanted to play cards.

"So, do you know?" he said.

"I know. I know, already."

"OK, so, where do babies come from?"

"From the doctor." Patrick made a mistake in the card game and got stuck picking up the whole pile.

"From the doctor?" Rex almost fell off the bed laughing.

"Well … every time Mom gets pregnant, it's always after she goes to the doctor. He must do something to her … some kind of operation."

"You don't know crap," Rex snorted. He put down his cards and got off the bed to peek in the hallway. Rex shut the door gently and closed the window halfway to quiet the storm, then got back on the bed.

"What?" Patrick whispered.

Rex told him everything. It's like baseball, he said. There's first base, then second, then third, and then a home run. That's where babies come from.

"Do you get it?" Rex asked.

Patrick was shot dead. Rex started to deal the cards again, but Patrick had lost all interest in cards. He got up and looked at a paint-by-numbers picture of a clown on the wall. Here was the hidden truth of the ages, something going on everywhere from the caveman days to the pyramids to America. Apparently, even Lincoln was involved. Adults everywhere were hiding it from kids while they tried to get to first base and beyond. Like a fool, Patrick had been spending his free time on the train tracks back home throwing rocks at empty soda bottles.

"Are you sure about this?" Patrick asked.

Suddenly, Rex's mom burst in the room without knocking. She was carrying an extra quilt which she threw over them like a fishing net.

"Mom!" Rex said. "You're wrecking our card game."

"Time for bed," she said, "but first I wanna fight the new kid."

"Fight? Not again."

"C'mon, Patrick, see if you can hit me," she said, holding up her fists. She was a big-chested mom with brown hair, a sunburned face, and clenched fists. Patrick looked over at Rex.

He shrugged. "She always does this when somebody new spends the night."

"Go ahead, just see if you can hit me," she said. "I won't hit you back."

Patrick got up slowly and took his stance. He tried a few jabs at her, but she blocked them, bobbing around, her chest bouncing inside her sailboat blouse.

"I don't *want* to hit you," he said, hopping left and right.

"Don't be a sissy. Just try. I wanna see wha'cha got!" she said. She was very tough for a mom.

Patrick pulled back his right hand and swung hard.

She ducked the punch, dove forward, and tackled him onto the bed. The mattress trampolined. Cards flew.

"Mom! You're crazy!" Rex yelled bouncing.

Patrick landed face down on the old quilt with Rex's mom keeping her weight on his back so he couldn't spring up and try again.

"You give up?" Her breath smelled like limes from her gin and tonic.

"Yeah," Patrick gasped. He had never known a mom like her.

She laughed, messed up Patrick's hair, and got up. She caught her breath and told him he did a good job. Then, turning to the mirror, she straightened her blouse and hair. Deep down, she wished she were a girl again, wrestling her little brothers and talking about monsters and ghosts. Those were some of her happiest times. But now she was forty and had to act right and talk about things like the weather and current events.

"Your father and I are going to watch the news and go to bed. They're getting ready for the moon launch this week. Patrick, isn't it great to be alive when we're going to the moon?"

"I guess."

"*You guess?* Why it's the fulfillment of a dream!" She looked at an empty wall as if she were watching President Kennedy give a speech. "Kennedy promised we're going to the moon before the end of the decade, and, *by God, we're going.* Now *there* was a man. You have to have some goal in this life, boys, or nothing happens." She drifted over to the window and cupped her face in her hands against the glass to see the storm and sighed. "I can't even see the lighthouse anymore. I don't know about tomorrow."

"What about breakfast?" Rex said.

"I don't know." She reeled around and checked her watch. "Be good and quiet, and maybe I'll make waffles." Rex's mom said goodnight, turned out the lamp, and left, closing the door behind her.

"Sorry about that," Rex said. "Is your mom crazy, too?"

"No, she's just always getting pregnant."

"Well, now you know why."

"Man."

The rain was marching across the roof, and Patrick lay on his back staring at the ceiling, thinking about his parents getting a home run to have another baby. It seemed unbelievable. There was nudity right in his own home.

"We should do something with our lives this trip," Rex said stretching out next to him.

"Like what?"

"Blow something up."

"No, I don't want to get arrested again."

"Again? You've never been arrested. Have you?"

Patrick didn't want to tell Rex everything about his past, like when he got caught robbing the Ben Franklin, or when he took some money from the safe at the bank during a Cub Scout trip, or when the railroad police chased him down the tracks for getting into box cars.

"I just made that up."

"Well, we should do something."

"Like what?"

Rex was quiet for a long while, thinking, and Patrick thought he had fallen asleep. Patrick was dozing off himself, listening to the storm, when he was jolted back with two words: "A contest!"

"What?"

"A contest … we should have a contest."

"What kind of contest?"

"A contest to see who can be the first to kiss a girl before the week is over."

Lightning flashed. The theme song to the evening news trumpeted through the floorboards. Impossible. Patrick didn't even answer. At school, it would take him a whole year just to talk to a girl. He didn't have that kind of confidence. Girls were mysterious, dangerous people. He'd learned the hard way. You may think a girl has that feeling for you—if you secretly have it for her—but you can be wrong. A girl can run you over like a freight train and leave you dead on the tracks. Kissing a girl takes years of preparation and study, like getting a driver's license. And a lot of guys fail parallel parking and have to take the test over. Kissing girls was a game for older boys—teenagers who shave chin hairs and use Ban Roll On. You can't just have a contest and do it in a week. Ridiculous. No way. Rex was waiting. Patrick had to pretend to be interested. "What would we win?"

Rex sat up excited. "*What would we win?* Why, just being able to say that we did it!"

"That's no contest without a prize." Patrick thought that would throw him off, but not Rex.

"All right, five dollars, if we have to have a prize."

"*Five bucks?* Maybe we should think about it."

"We'll get started tomorrow." Rex lay down and talked some more about how to walk up to girls they didn't know and get them interested. He went on and on and on. Patrick rolled over with his back to Rex. When Patrick wasn't answering back, Rex switched it over to the Mothman to see if he was awake or not. Patrick pretended to be really tired. His eyes were closed, but he was listening to how Mothman operates—how he flies in and tiptoes up to people. The rain was tapping on the leaves in the dark woods behind the cottage, disguising any footsteps that might be out there. Rex got quiet, and after a while Patrick heard him breathing heavier. He was asleep. Patrick listened to the storm outside and decided he needed to set some goal for the trip, like President Kennedy had set for the moon. He decided Rex was right. Before the trip was over he would try to kiss a girl, any girl.

# - chapter four -

SOMBER ORGAN music echoed off the marble walls and statues as Patrick and his family arrived late for Mass. It was the morning before the sleepover, before he had met Rex and learned the truth about baseball. For Patrick the day had begun with the banging of pots and pans, his mother awakening an exhausted family to get ready for church. Even though they were on vacation and a lake view beckoned them to indolence on their first day, there was no escaping God. Mom made sure of it. Coaxing children from bed with the promise of breakfast, she served up only burnt toast with hunks of butter left over from the last people who rented the cottage. Then she double-timed them back into the station wagon, only to arrive halfway through the first song when all the good seats in back where no one would notice them were already taken. Just like home.

Dad led the family toward St. Patrick Church's front row as everyone followed—John, Patrick, Teddy, Elizabeth, and Mom with baby Joey in her arms. They genuflected then knelt to say a prayer. Patrick was too trouble-free to pray, so he looked at all the strangers. They had the same uncertain look on their faces as the people back home. Everyone stood, and the priest told them to think up any sins they had committed. The crowd shifted, rubbing noses, clearing throats. Patrick was only half listening, but right away that magazine with the naked women blazed in his mind. White round bottoms. Full breasts. He tried to distract his conscience by looking around and saw Dad looking into the distance. What is he thinking? Patrick wondered. Dad never told anyone what was on his mind during Mass, but sometimes he would get the same serious look in church that he got the night before income taxes were due. And that made Patrick feel gloomy. That and the fact that the weather was threatening. How were they going to have fun at the beach if it rained?

"Vacation," the priest said as if warning of riptides ahead. "Most of you have only seven days, just as in life we have only seven decades."

"It's going to storm," Mom leaned over and whispered to Dad. Dad looked at his watch. Patrick looked everywhere but at the priest. He didn't like sermons and tried not to listen.

The priest paused to tap his fingernails on the oak podium and scan the crowd with a lifeguard gaze. Then he got going and bobbed his head around making his white hair that needed a trim toss up like lake foam on a red flag day. "At first, you think it's going to be a long trip. You think you can enjoy the fun forever, but before you know it, it's Wednesday. You're forty. It's Thursday. You're fifty. All of a sudden, it's Friday and you have to face your dirty laundry. My God, you think, I'm sixty! How can this be? I haven't lived! I used to be young. What happened? All that's left is the long, hot drive home. You have to say goodbye to the beach, and you feel so unprepared to leave … it brings a pang to your heart, and why?"

Taking a breath, the priest calmed down his hair and smoothed out his sermon notes. Everyone waited. Thunder rumbled, and lightning stabbed at the church. Through the open stained glass windows, Patrick could see a river of rain running down the blacktop parking lot. Vacationers from all over the Midwest waited to hear what the priest would say next while trying not to be caught looking out the window.

"BECAUSE YOU NEVER BELIEVED IT WOULD COME!" he finally bellowed.

Of all the dumb comparisons, Patrick thought. Life wasn't like that at all. It's way longer than a week. A week was nothing. Patrick had been grounded for a week in his room, and with the radio, comic books, and a model airplane to build, it wasn't so bad. A week could go by easy. But life takes forever. Everybody always has plenty of time, Patrick thought, and the old people about to die only got that way after many long years that went slow. Dad was leaning forward listening intently, and Patrick tried to listen for faults in the sermon he could pick apart later in case he was asked about it. The storm rumbled outside, and a big flash of lightning hit a tree on the side lawn. *BOOM!* A branch fell and clipped a wire. The church went dark. Women shrieked. Babies cried. Dad checked for his wallet. Patrick sat up straight. The priest motioned to stay calm and tried to finish the sermon, but his microphone was dead, and he lost control. Parishioners got up and ran for the basement. It was like the Japanese monster movie *Mothra,* with people fleeing the city in fear.

"We've got to get back to the cottage," Dad said to Mom.

"No wait, we should stay here where it's safe," Mom said.

"We can't waste any time," Dad said. "We're on vacation."

The Cantwells dashed through the downpour into the parking lot. A live wire by the tree limb that had fallen was smoking and hissing in the grass. The kids hopped in the car and dried their hair with their shirts as Dad started the engine and gunned it. Smoke shot out the tailpipe, and he flipped on the windshield wipers and raced out of the parking lot.

*"Slow down!"* Mom yelled.

"You heard what he told us," Dad shouted as the station wagon bounced and splashed down the rain-slick road. We've only got a week!" He looked in the rearview mirror at his offspring. "Listen, everyone. We only have a week. We're going to plan out this trip and do as much as we can. You understand?"

Everyone nodded or said OK.

"No sleeping late or wasting time. We've got to *live* this trip and make every day count like it's our last vacation together."

Mom screamed. Dad looked forward and slammed on the brakes. He had run a red light just as a headstone delivery truck was passing through the intersection with another shipment bound for the cemetery. The front of the station wagon missed the truck by inches.

"*Jayzul,* we have got to wake up as a family," Dad said. He drove immediately to Meijer's grocery store, and everyone tromped through the puddles and went inside. A modern supermarket, Meijer's had bright lights and air conditioning. Overhead speakers played the song "Shangri la." It was a comforting ballad about a place securely anchored in the here and now, a land of flowers and blue birds and nothing to do. Everyone felt better. They shivered through the frozen food aisle, loading up the shopping cart with bacon, ground beef, chicken, potatoes, soda, milk, orange juice, eggs, pancake mix, Mrs. Butterworth's syrup, blueberries, bread, ice cream, butter, Cap'n Crunch, Cheerios, CHEEZ-ITS, bologna, pickle loaf, apples, bananas, and Chips Ahoy cookies—everything they would need to make the trip last. Throughout the store, Meijer's stock boys jogged the aisles replacing products taken from the shelves with identical boxes as if the food supply—and the present moment—would go on forever.

"This store is a triumph of civilization," Dad told a stock boy. The stock boy nodded and pulled the trigger on a price sticker gun to mark another box of Rice-A-Roni.

At the checkout line, Patrick watched the mountain of groceries move forward on the conveyer belt and thought about how he needed to do something BIG on the trip, something that mattered, before all the groceries were eaten and it was time to go back home. At the time he felt something was coming, but he didn't know what yet. Dad and Mom were distracted, talking with someone behind them in line, so Patrick grabbed a jumbo pack of Juicy Fruit gum without permission and threw it on the conveyer belt. Just then Mom called out to him.

"Hey, Patrick," she said, "I want you to meet some friends of ours from St. Louis. Their son's in the same grade as you."

Patrick looked back. It was Rex. He was holding a *Mad* magazine and peering over the top like Alfred E. Neuman.

# - chapter five -

MONDAY MORNING Patrick woke up in the bed next to Rex and looked out the window. The sun was shining against a brilliant blue sky, and in the distance, the lake was calm and flat. Fishermen with straw hats looked like dabs of color on a painting as their lines disappeared into the blue-green water resting snug along the pier. The lighthouse and fog house were bright red. A few boats sat on the horizon, their sails like white triangles against the blue. He thought about kissing a girl, and wondered if the project would get going today.

"Rex, it's morning."

They got dressed and went downstairs. No one else was up except Rex's big dog, Clyde. They let Clyde out to pee and took in the weather. A black squirrel saw the dog and ran into the woods behind the cottage with Clyde in hot pursuit. Beach towels that had been blown off the line in the storm lay on the wet, sandy yard. But the day was sunny and easy, and Patrick was happy.

"Looks like a green flag day," Rex growled. "No good waves."

After he peed, the dog came right back in for breakfast. Rex put a scoop of dry dog food in one bowl and some fresh water in the other, then opened the refrigerator and leaned on the door looking in.

"Crap, there's nothing to eat in this place."

"Your mom said she'd make waffles."

"We might die waiting."

Rex got out some milk and drank straight from the bottle with his mouth, not caring about spreading germs, and then gave Patrick the bottle. He drank some, too, and gave it back to Rex to put away. Rex took another swig, set it down on the counter, and left the top off. Reaching for a block of Kraft American Cheese on the fridge door, Rex peeled off a slice and took a bite. He gave the block to Patrick who peeled off a piece, too. They left the cheese out on the counter unwrapped, and went into the living room, because Rex had something secret he wanted to show Patrick. With no one around, Rex reached up on the bookshelf and pulled down the World Book Encyclopedia, volume "S."

"What is it?" Patrick said.

"Shhhh, look up what I was telling you. It's all in here," Rex said.

"What's it under?" Patrick said, opening the volume to an article on sea turtles.

"You don't know anything." Rex took the book and walked out onto the screened porch, leafing through to the right page. "Here, read this."

Patrick sat down on a wicker sofa while Rex kept a lookout, tossing the dog a cheese scrap. "Good boy, good Clyde."

Patrick looked at the illustration of a naked man and woman and read the explanation of where babies come from. The article called it "sexual reproduction." There was no mention of first base or home runs, but it was pretty much true to what Rex had told him.

"No wonder their bedroom door is locked."

Across the way and up on a hill, a screen door banged. Rex's head jerked. They heard a tiny *yarf* of a dog bark that set Clyde to barking good and loud. Rex shushed him right away.

"Quick, get the binoculars!"

"What for?"

"Hurry. It's *her*."

"Who?"

"Hurry!"

Patrick ran tiptoe upstairs, grabbed Rex's flying saucer binoculars, and came back down. Rex was spying out the living room window at someone.

"Gimmie."

He handed over the binoculars, and Rex looked through the window. Up on the hill by a yellow cottage across the way was a blonde girl with her dog. She was too far away for Patrick to see her face. It was like sitting in the free seats at the Muny Opera in St. Louis where the actors singing *Oklahoma* look like stick people until you get your turn with the binoculars.

# Try to Kiss a Girl

"There she is again," Rex said.

"Who?"

"The girl from Indiana."

"You know her?"

"No, but I seen her plates when she came with her mom. And then she got out of the car, first her legs and then … *the rest of her.*"

"Let me see."

"She's too old for you."

Rex was hogging the binoculars, so Patrick lost interest and looked around the room. Above the fireplace was a varnished, wooden clipper ship model with cloth sails and threaded riggings and little hand-painted sailors on the deck. The original cottage owner had worked long hours making it on his deathbed. He wanted to leave behind something that would last forever. A handwritten sign by the ship warned: "For display only. Please don't put in the lake." Over in the corner on a table, there was a small TV set with a big antenna. Facing the TV was a pair of wicker chairs with green cushions that had butt craters from Rex's parents watching the astronauts getting ready to go to the moon. Two grownup glasses were on the coffee table—an empty one with a lime and lipstick marks, and a half-empty one that smelled of whiskey. Rex's dad had a big job selling stocks, and a stock market page of the newspaper lay open on the floor with little numbers circled.

"Here, look," Rex said.

Patrick peered through the eyeholes, and there she was—with long, blonde hair, a white T-shirt, yellow shorts, long tan legs and bare feet. Her face was beautiful but a little sad.

"Have you noticed her nose?" Rex said.

"What about it?"

"It's so perfect. If I could pick any nose on a girl, I'd pick hers."

"Gross."

"You know what I mean. What's she doing now?"

"She's just standing there with her hand on her hips, whistling. No, wait, now she's bending over to get her dog."

"Quick, this is the good part."

Rex grabbed back the binoculars and gave a description of everything. "Whenever she picks up that dumb dog … Oh, there she goes. *Mannnnnnn* … She's just kissing that dog right on the lips, over and over and over again. God! That dog has the life."

"Let me see."

"No way."

Patrick tried to see from the window, but without binoculars, she was just a faraway girl. Nothing special at all.

"Now what?"

"She's going inside, here."

Patrick looked again real fast, but she was going back inside, and the screen door banged behind her.

"How old is she?"

"I don't know, maybe fifteen."

"We'll never be that old."

"I know, but there's other girls."

"Who?"

"These two girls more our age down at the Khardomah."

"You know them?"

"Well, they walked by once."

"Did you talk to them?"

"Sort of. I fired a bottle rocket at them."

"You fired a bottle rocket at girls?"

"Not *at* them, just near them."

"Why'd you do that?"

"To say hi."

"What'd they say?"

"They ran off. But I could tell they were interested."

"Rex, that's no way—"

"It was just the start. Next thing we'll do is—"

Clyde started woofing again, and the boys looked up to see Patrick's dad walking in the sunlight along the side of the cottage toward the screen door. Behind him was the Buick station wagon with John and Teddy hanging out the windows. Rex and Patrick looked at each other and both said it at the same time.

"THE ENCYCLOPEDIA!"

It was still sitting on the porch open to the page on sexual reproduction with all the naked pictures and diagrams. They shot onto the screened porch, sliding on the throw rug as they went. Rex grabbed the encyclopedia, slammed it shut, and slid it halfway under a rocking chair cushion. Dad knocked on the screen door and peered in.

"Boys, what's going on? Permission to come aboard?"

"Hi, Dad," Patrick said, wishing he could get another look at the pictures before he had to leave.

Rex's dog barked at Dad. "Clyde! Shhhhhh!" Rex grabbed Clyde and held him back.

"Sorry to come by so early," he said to Patrick, "but I'm taking you and your brothers fishing."

"Fishing?" Patrick said, looking at Rex. "Can he come, too?"

"Well, I'm afraid it's a small boat," Dad said, studying Rex, scanning the room. His eyes narrowed on the encyclopedia volume "S" protruding slightly from the pillow. "Maybe some other time. Now, get your things and let's go."

"All right." Patrick ran back upstairs for his pajamas and toothbrush and then followed Dad out. "I'll see you around, Rex. Thanks for having me over."

A squeaky spring pulled the screen door shut with a bang, and Patrick felt like a little kid being dragged off to a family car ride while the whole town was just jumping with girls.

"I'll see you around, "Rex called out. "We'll play some *baseball* this trip."

Dad shot Patrick a look as they walked out to the station wagon. He knew Patrick didn't like baseball, and, like all dads, he also knew the secret of what baseball really meant. He studied Patrick's face as they climbed in the car. Patrick slid in the back next to Teddy who, like John in the front seat, was still half asleep. Patrick avoided Dad's gaze and looked back at the yellow cottage on the hill as the car pulled away. But there was no sign of the girl from Indiana.

# - chapter six -

PATRICK STUDIED the faces of people they passed as they drove through Grand Haven toward Spring Lake. Did they all know *the secret?* How could he have been so blind? How could he have gone *his whole life* without knowing? He couldn't wait to tell John he was in on it now, too. He wanted to find out if there was anything else he'd been missing, anything else everyone but him and a bunch of other little kids knew. But he wasn't going to get a chance to talk for a while since John was in the front seat fiddling with the radio dial, trying to find a Beatle's song, and Patrick was stuck next to Teddy, who was eight years old and only knew Santa Claus lived at the North Pole and Bob Gibson pitched for the Cardinals. Unlike Patrick when he was eight, Teddy was a good kid who liked little league and never went up on the tracks to hop trains or throw rocks at buses or get arrested.

Once they got to Spring Lake, which was about five-minutes inland from Grand Haven, they walked into a bayou diner next to the bait shop. They stood on the edge of the diner floor holding tackle boxes and fishing poles while a counter full of local men ate fried eggs, smoked, and laughed. They all knew the secret; Patrick could tell. Before he knew it, Patrick would have only noticed the smell of bacon and eggs and pancake syrup and coffee. Before, he would have only wanted breakfast. But now he studied their faces—their teasing jabs at each other, their hurricane laughter and wide smiles—and wondered how many of them were so happy because they had a home run last night.

When Dad saw the local men, he squinted his eyes and got that *How-could-*

*anyone-smoke-in-this-day-and-age?* look on his face. That was the question Dad always posed to the boys whenever he saw people smoking. But not in front of smokers, always privately so only the boys could hear. *Don't they know what the Surgeon General found?* Dad would ask as he imagined the men's laughter turning to coughing fits and hospital days and all-consuming cancer. He shook his head at the thought that in five or ten years some of the diner stools would be empty as those men would be laid out in their best Sunday suits with a good six feet of dirt on top of them, unable to order ham and eggs or take their kids fishing forever. That's how Dad felt about people smoking. "They're killing themselves by inches," he preached to the boys.

Patrick also noticed the smoke and wished he could have a cigarette. But he had quit. It had been a whole two days now.

"Can we eat breakfast here?" Teddy asked.

"Not today," Dad said. He got out a breath mint, turned his back on the breakfast counter, and walked into the adjoining bait shop. "Follow me, boys."

The bait shop was a cool, humid shrine of fishing hopes and dreams, bubbling with minnow tanks, chirping with crickets kept warm in lamp-lit aquariums. The minnows and crickets had no idea of the pointy hooks, dark lake, and fish mouths in their future. John and Patrick had been fishing with Dad before and had their own equipment, but this was the first time for Teddy, and he needed a pole. The boys followed Dad down an aisle lined with four-dollar bass lures dangling from peg hooks, which he said were "a racket," then around a corner to grab a plastic bag of pinch-on lead weights. Dad chose a packet of snells and a few red-and-white bobbers and came to stop in front of a barrel of cane poles.

"What do you think, Teddy?" Dad asked.

The boys all looked at the cane poles.

"I want a *real* pole," Teddy said, "not a baby one."

Dad looked around. "Teddy, I'll tell you what I'm gonna do," he said using his downtown executive voice. "I'll get you a good pole, since this is your first fishing trip. But you have to take care of it."

"OK," Teddy said.

"A good fishing pole will last a lifetime."

"OK."

Dad reached up high and pulled down a Zebco rod and reel marked $17.50 and handed it to Teddy. Teddy couldn't believe it. John and Patrick couldn't believe it. It was way better than the rod and reels they had.

"Thanks, Dad!"

"Does this mean we can get some pancakes or something?" Patrick said.

"No, just doughnuts and milk. Let's go fishing!" Dad said.

Dad paid for all the stuff and rented the boat. The man behind the counter tried to sell Dad fishing licenses, but he didn't want to spend the extra money.

"I hope the sheriff don't catch you," the man said.

"Nothing bad can happen. We're on vacation, and we're living life," Dad said as he patted Teddy on the head. "Right, boys?"

They piled into the wooden skiff with white, flakey paint and sat on three benches. The little boat rocked left and right in the water. Dad put on his orange life jacket, and the boys put on theirs. The red-faced bait shop man with a cigarette on his lip leaned over to show Dad how to start the engine like a lawn mower with a rope he would have to pull. With a great grunt, he handed Dad the anchor, an Old Judge coffee can full of cement with a long rope coming out the top, and then pushed them away from the dock at the end of which sat a barefoot boy with blond hair holding a clumsy cane pole. He was just a local kid, not on vacation, and Patrick felt sorry for him. With no boat, no Dad along, and no Zebco pole, he had no hope of catching real fish. Patrick almost wished they could invite him along, but then Dad pulled the ripcord, the engine came alive, and Patrick forgot all about him.

"Here we go!" Dad hollered.

Blue smoke coughed from the stern as the propeller churned the water. The bait shop man waved. The bow rose up as the boat cut across the bayou full of lily pads. Everyone was happy and quiet with reverence for this moment of escape from the shore. The shore was bad because it connected to the road that led to the highway, which led to St. Louis, which led to their school desks and nuns and to Dad's desk and his boss. Before them lay deep water and freedom. There could be perch, bass, carp, catfish, and northern pike with sharp teeth down below, all waiting to be caught. Dad let go a wild *yalp*, a kind of Indian chant from his boyhood days in Michigan that the boys had never heard before.

"*Hick*-tah-minnicka-hannicka-sock-tah-*boom*-tah-*lay* ... *Yoo hoo!*"

"What's that?" John said.

"That's the secret Indian saying for us to catch a lot of fish," Dad said. "My Pop used to say that when I was a boy up here."

To think that Dad had once been a kid on vacation in the same place made it almost seem possible that Patrick could get old. But that was higher than algebra to understand, and he quickly put it out of his mind. "Does it work?"

Patrick asked.

"Every time. Let's eat our doughnuts first, before we get worm germs on our hands."

They ate fast, enjoying Holland Cream long johns and milk, as the boat chugged across the lake to an inviting cove shaded by an overhanging weeping willow tree. Dad cut the engine, and John let down the coffee can anchor. The rope attached to the anchor zoomed into the water as bubbles floated to the top, just like in the movie *The Creature from the Black Lagoon*.

"OK," Dad whispered, "now we have to be quiet so we don't scare the fish away."

The boys nodded. It was time to bait their hooks and cast into the water and wait.

This was it.

Everyone was quiet.

They waited.

Nothing happened.

They kept quiet another long stretch.

"Maybe I should recast," Teddy said.

"Shhh," Dad whispered. "Just be patient."

So they waited some more watching their bobbers and hoping. Any second now, a bobber could disappear as a giant fish chomped on the hook down in the deep.

On the shore road a red pickup truck playing country music banjoed on by trailing dust. The truck and the song slipped around the bend, and the dust settled. Bobbers drifted. The sun warmed their backs. "What was that Indian saying again?" Patrick said.

"*Hick*-tah-minnicka-hannicka-sock-tah-*boom*-tah-*lay* ... *Yoo hoo!*" Dad said.

The boys all tried to say it softly together. Their lips were all moving, but it wasn't working. Dad reeled in and pulled the ripcord to start the engine. It took a few pulls and he was getting aggravated. They sputtered around the lake getting snagged and hot and discouraged, until a big boat came by with some local men on the deck holding up a stringer of fat fish with silvery scales shining in the sun.

"WHERE'D YOU CATCH THEM?" Dad called out.

"WHAT?"

"WHERE'D YOU CATCH THOSE FISH?" he called louder.

"BY THE BRIDGE," the man yelled pointing behind him.

"Of course," Dad said. "Pull up anchor. We should have thought of that. Fish like structure." He started the engine again, and they rode a great distance to the big bridge, where Spring Lake empties into the Grand River on its way to Lake Michigan. They were putting their hands in the water to cool off, but Dad kidded them that a northern pike might bite them, so they jerked their fingers in and tried to see down into the dark water where finger-eating fish were following them just waiting for a chance. Arriving at the bridge, they re-baited to get ready. John was just about to drop anchor when Dad noticed an official boat approaching. It was the sheriff. He was on patrol looking for violations.

"Quick, hide your poles," Dad said, "Act like we're sightseeing."

Gunning the engine, Dad maneuvered the boat under the bridge. Teddy saw the flash of a fish in the water and tried to cast for it. But his new Zebco, with its factory-fresh lubricated gears, threw the line way up in the sky, hooking onto the metal beams under the bridge. Just then an orange light on the bridge deck started flashing, and they all looked around. A large coal tanker was bearing down on them, approaching the bridge. It was a drawbridge.

"Quick, reel in your line!" Dad said. "We've got to get out of here!"

"It's stuck!" Teddy said.

"Help your brother!" Dad said to the older boys.

Patrick grabbed Teddy's Zebco as John fumbled with the line, trying to unsnag it from the bridge, but it was hooked solid. The Sheriff noticed the small skiff in the channel in the path of the approaching tanker.

"CLEAR THE CHANNEL. CLEAR THE CHANNEL IMMEDIATELY," the sheriff called over a megaphone.

Dad turned the boat about, and the Zebco shot from Patrick's hands. Teddy started crying. The rising drawbridge lifted up the $17.50 rod and reel in the air, swinging above the channel.

"It's OK, we'll get it after the boat passes," Dad said.

A coal ship as tall as a building slid under the lifted drawbridge. Dad and the boys held onto the sides of the skiff as it rocked in the wake. A deck hand on the cargo ship came out of a cabin door and lit a cigarette with his head down. The dangling Zebco struck him from behind on the shoulder. Turning around, he wrestled his attacker, pulling the rod and reel free. Dad yelled, *HEY, THAT BELONGS TO MY SON!* But the deck hand couldn't hear him over the engine. He wiped off the rod and reel with his shirt and hurried back below to show his shipmates his good fortune.

They watched the tanker slide away, as the sheriff's boat passed by going the other way.

"Tell the sheriff to go after him and get my reel," Teddy said.

"I'd better not," Dad said, "We don't have a fishing license."

Sad and defeated, they chugged back to the bait shop dock. As they threw anchor on land and got out, the blond boy with the cane pole walked past them with a stringer heavy with perch and blue gill. Dad gave him some money for the fish, and the kid ran off happy. Then Dad handed Patrick the fish.

"What are these for?" he asked.

"We have to have something to show your mother."

John and Patrick waited in the car while Dad went back in the bait shop with Teddy. Teddy was mopey walking in, then happy walking out. Dad had bought him another Zebco.

"We have a good dad," John said.

"I know." Patrick and John watched Dad and Teddy walking toward the car.

"But he seems different this trip," John said.

"Maybe it's downtown," Patrick said.

"I never want to work downtown."

The car door opened, and Teddy and Dad got in. Dad turned and looked them all square in the eye. "Boys, we won't tell anybody what happened to us, and they won't know. You understand?"

"OK," they said.

"If anyone asks how we did, just say we had a great time fishing."

# - chapter seven -

STEINER'S DRUG STORE dispensed products to postpone death and prolong a vanishing thing called *now*. To the wandering customer, the entire store promised that life was reliable —from the tile floor speckled with atomic particle shapes representing all the microscopic secrets science had discovered to fight disease, to the rows of skin softeners, lotions, balms, ointments, hair dye, vitamins, and blackhead removal kits promising beauty and endless tomorrows. The air smelled healthy and nourishing, with grilled cheese sandwiches, hamburgers, and frankfurters cooking behind the lunch counter where customers sat on swivel stools watching the waitress ladle up hot fudge, butterscotch, or marshmallow sauce onto ice cream sundaes. The bald druggist with thick, black-framed glasses and a mint green, short-sleeved shirt counted pills with a butter knife while Dad asked him where the itchy bottom powder was. Dashing into Steiner's had been Dad's idea, an impulse after the fishing trip, to search for some vague product—what he didn't know—to feel more confident of life. While Dad looked around, John studied a modeling clay kit, Teddy looked at a *Sports Illustrated*, and Patrick stood by the penny fortune scale twirling the postcard rack. He grabbed a postcard of girls water skiing in bikinis and then fumbled it on the floor when he heard a "Pssssst" right next to his ear. Whirling around, he found Rex behind him, pointing at the next aisle over.

"She's over there!" he whispered.

"Who?"

"The girl you're gonna kiss before the trip's over."

Patrick peeked around the Coppertone display and saw them. Two girls standing there, just a few feet away, smiling and talking and looking at something he couldn't see. They were both lovely. "Which one?"

"I don't care. You take one, and I'll take the other. You go left, I'll go right. You go up, I'll go down."

Patrick looked again and noticed one of them was sleepy-eyed with curly, shoulder-length, blonde hair and a ready-to-yawn look on her face, as if she'd spent half the morning in front of the mirror combing her hair and it wore her out. Patrick watched her uncap a ChapStick and rub some on her lips. The other girl had black hair pulled back in a ponytail and long bangs. She was pretty, too. The black-haired one talked fast and bossy and kept uncapping bottles, whiffing lotions, and wrinkling her nose like she was unhappy with the scent of life so far.

"I like the sleepy-looking one," Patrick said.

"Shhhh, that's Tammy. No, I'm wrong, that's Ginny."

"Are you sure? Did you talk to them?"

"We haven't met yet. You go talk to them first."

"What?"

"It's okay. They're nice. I've been following them and spy listening."

Just then, Patrick's Dad came along humming "St. James Infirmary," a song from his high school days. In his hands, he held a fresh pack of downtown breath mints and a canister of itchy bottom powder. Patrick and Rex reeled around and looked at him.

"Why, Rex, what are you doing here? Where are your folks?"

"Oh, they're back at the cottage, I guess. How was fishing, Mr. Cantwell?"

Patrick listened to see if Dad would tell a lie, but he told the truth.

"Oh, we had a great outing. The car's full of fish." He turned to Patrick. "Listen, I'm getting John some modeling clay, so he can work on an art project and accomplish something this trip. You want anything?"

He looked at the girls. "I don't know."

"Well, think of something you want, and then we have to go. Here." He handed Patrick the itchy bottom powder to free his hands, and left. Rex waited until Mr. Cantwell had disappeared and then pushed Patrick toward the girls.

"Hi," Patrick said.

The girls looked at him, and at the itchy bottom powder, and then at each other and back at him.

"I'm Patrick."

They told him their names, Tammy and Ginny. Then, Tammy—the one he wasn't supposed to kiss—started talking about how they were school friends from Atlanta. Ginny stretched her arm and half yawned. She said it was sure "dreadfully hot" in Atlanta. Patrick nodded. "We come up here to get away from the heat," Tammy said. "It's burning hot in Atlanta." They had southern accents that made ballads out of everything they said. It was relaxing listening to them, but Patrick had to be careful not to let the music muffle the words and leave him with nothing to say back. Girls back in St. Louis talked flat and nasally with no melody in their voices to get you all carried away. It was much easier to talk to St. Louis girls, but not nearly as interesting. While Tammy was talking, Ginny went after her ChapStick again, and Patrick watched her smooth another coating on her lips. He wanted to kiss her right then and there. He could almost imagine it, leaning over just so and ... then he noticed both girls staring at him. Daydreaming so, he missed a beat where he should have said something to fill the dead space. The girls waited. It was his turn to say something, anything. His mind scrambled, tripping over itself trying to think of something interesting, but all he could think of was something he'd heard Dad say about Atlanta. Dad was a history buff who was always teaching them stuff about the past.

"I hear General Sherman burned Atlanta."

It got quiet. Tammy took a step back, and Ginny just cracked her neck, bored. It was so quiet Patrick could hear the malt maker in back cutting through a scoop of ice cream, and traffic out on the street as the front door swung open and closed.

"I'm Rex!" Suddenly Rex was upon them, swooping in unseen, like Mothman attacking unsuspecting campers in the woods. *Whew!* Patrick was relieved, but Rex looked tense. His smile was big and fake—the kind of smile some kids have on school picture day. Those were the kids whose moms always yelled at them when their picture arrived, but then would hang it on the dining room wall where relatives would see it over Thanksgiving and feel sorry for them.

"You following us?" Tammy asked.

"Why, no," Rex said.

"You're the one shooting off those fireworks! Aiming at us on purpose!"

"Me? No, I was just lighting them off and one got away. Me and Patrick are on vacation. We're vacation friends."

"We're from St. Louis," Patrick said, swallowing.

"Why you following us?" Tammy demanded. Her eyes were confident and brown, the color of hot fudge.

Rex pretended to look with interest at a row of Dr. Scholl's sensitive toe separator pads hanging on pegs while he kept talking, looking sideways at them every few words. "We thought maybe you might want to meet us at the beach sometime and go swimming."

Tammy drew in a breath, ready to exhale a *NO*—maybe because Sherman had burned Atlanta, or maybe because of Rex's fireworks. But before she could breathe out, Ginny looked Patrick in the eyes. Her eyes were spring green, like some potion the pharmacist would mix on a snowy night and wrap in paper and then have rushed by delivery truck to a house so a feverish boy could get well.

"I'll go," Ginny said.

"That's great," Rex said, and he stuck out his hand to shake on it before they could change their minds. Patrick blinked to get away from Ginny's eyes, but found himself staring at her lips instead. He could see every puffy, pillowy patch coated with ChapStick goodness and shine. Tammy saw Patrick memorizing Ginny's lips and struck out at him.

"What've you got itchy bottom powder for?" she said backhanding the canister. "Is your butt burning?"

Everyone laughed at Patrick, and he felt his face get warm.

"Ha! You're blushing!" Tammy laughed.

Ginny and Rex laughed, too.

Patrick could have jumped in and corrected her. He could have gotten mad and said, *Why no, Tammy, it's not for me; it's for my dad or baby Joey.* But sometimes it was OK to be the butt of a joke and suffer everyone laughing at him, if it would help move things along. To get ready for the moon, the astronauts had to spin around in the practice capsule and throw up scrambled eggs plenty of times. Trying to kiss a girl was just like practicing for space, so he let them laugh and tried to laugh along with them. Then they all agreed to meet up later at the beach by the State Park Pavilion.

"Hey, Patrick?"

He turned to see Dad signal with a raised eyebrow and a tilt of his head to come quickly. Patrick said goodbye and went to get in line with John and Teddy. As Dad paid, he looked down at Patrick.

"What are you doing talking to girls? I didn't talk to a girl until I was in high school."

Patrick shrugged.

Dad asked him again what he wanted him to buy. "Isn't there anything special you want this trip?" Patrick looked around and saw the cigarettes. What he really wanted was a pack of Camel non-filters, the kind he and friends had smoked back home on the tracks after they watched a Humphrey Bogart movie. Bogart would have known how to talk to Ginny and kiss her before the week was out. But Patrick had to settle for another pack of Juicy Fruit. The jumbo pack he got at Meijer's was still on his dresser back at the cottage. There was no such thing as too much gum on vacation when you can't smoke.

Patrick was feeling pretty good once they got outside into the sunlight. He had a date on the beach and the whole week ahead of him. But then John gave out a moan, and he turned to see why. DOOM! In the window was a Back to School display of pens, pencils notebooks, and crayons. Back to school? This was only July. But already school authorities and the retail industry were plotting the recapture of children everywhere. Patrick thought of his classroom back at Mary Queen of Our Hearts. It was waiting for him with straight rows of empty desks, stale *National Geographics* baking on the bookshelf, and slanting slabs of sunlight from the windows inching across the floor toward September. He could hear the schoolroom clock ticking. Dad saw the boys' faces.

"Don't worry, boys, we still have all week."

They piled back in the station wagon with the dead fish and headed to the cottage.

# - chapter eight -

HOW TO KISS A GIRL for the first time? During their sleepover, Rex had told Patrick that he needed a plan—a trick—to get a girl to like him so she would feel *she* wanted to kiss *him*. "She has to think you don't care either way," Rex said, flexing his skinny arm muscle in the mirror. "You're only doing it for her." First, they would have to go to the beach and find Tammy and Ginny and then spend some time with them, pretending to have fun. And later, they'd probably have to spend some money on the girls for food or a movie. It was a big project. It might have to go in phases with the first part being the beach, and then maybe they'd meet up again at Dairy Treat or on the lookout to watch the sunset over the lake.

"Sunsets are very powerful with girls," Rex had said.

"I know," Patrick had said.

"You know? How do you know anything about it?"

"I know some. I saw on that show *Love American Style* that all our babysitters watch, they have lots of kissing at sunset."

"You still have babysitters?"

"Not for me. It's for my little brother and diapers. I know about kissing at sunset."

"That's when we'll do it then."

"I'd rather do it at sunrise."

"Sunrise?"

"Yeah, sunrises are better, because with a sunset, you feel robbed that the

EFFERSON COUNTY LIBRARY
NORTHWEST BRANCH

day is gone, and it's almost time for taking a bath or going to bed."

"No, no, no … that won't work. No girl likes a sunrise. They're all asleep in a room full of Barbie dolls and candy wrappers. You'd never get a girl awake in time to kiss her at a sunrise. And if you did, you both might have bad breath and wreck it."

Rex's advice was replaying through Patrick's mind when he got back to the cottage. All he wanted to do was grab a quick lunch and put on his swimming suit and head to the beach.

"What smells?" Mom said.

Dad glanced at the boys in the kitchen where they had the dead fish in the sink. His eyes glinted to remind them of *the secret* of how they bought the fish and didn't really catch them. Mom walked in the kitchen, holding baby Joey, and saw the pile of fish.

"Wow, looks like you had a good morning," she said.

Something about her voice said she *didn't* have a good morning.

"What's wrong? Is the pipe still leaking?" Dad said.

The upstairs bathroom pipe was still dripping all over the floor, she said. And Mom had walked down to Rex's cottage to ask his mom to call a plumber. There was no phone at Patrick's cottage. But that wasn't it. Something was wrong with Elizabeth. With her voice almost crying, Mom said Elizabeth might have appendicitis or a ruptured spleen because she was crunched up in a ball on the bed holding her abdomen, crying.

"I don't know what to give her," Mom said.

"We need to go the hospital," Dad said.

"Are you sure?"

"Let's not take any chances."

Dad looked at Teddy. Once when Teddy was little, Dad had saved his life by rushing him to the hospital when he had a bad fever. At the time, Mom had wanted to wait until morning. But Dad said, no, let's go now. Turned out Teddy had meningitis. After that, whenever one of the kids was in bed with a high fever, or bleeding with cut fingers from whittling a pinewood derby car the wrong way, Dad was always for going to the hospital. Right away, the boys threw the stringer of dead fish in the freezer, and Dad ran upstairs to pick up Elizabeth in her blanket and carry her down to the car. Mom hurried out, too, and John and Teddy got in the car. Patrick straggled out last and stood by the hood.

"Get in," Mom said.

"What about the beach?" It was a selfish thing to even think, and he felt guilty as soon as he heard himself say it. But he wasn't a doctor. They didn't need him along. He could be down at the beach with Rex getting busy with his own project. He only had a week.

*"Patrick!"* Dad said. "Your sister is sick! *Get in.*"

So he got in. The station wagon zoomed off—away from the cottage, away from the beach, away from Tammy and Ginny—through the pine tree-lined woods to the Grand Haven hospital. In the way back seat, Patrick could see the sun flashing through the treetops—ancient, tall pines that had seen a lot of winters and summers with other cars racing under them to the hospital. The station wagon engine was roaring serious. Wind was blowing through the open windows. Nobody talked. The car lurched to a stop at the emergency room door, and Mom got out with Elizabeth in her arms.

"Say a prayer," she said slamming the car door with her butt.

Dad squealed into a parking spot and jumped out, popping a downtown breath mint in his mouth as he went. *"Let's move,"* he ordered as he picked up baby Joey. The rest of them got out fast. From his face, they could see Dad was in a decisive mood. He snapped his fingers at Patrick for forgetting to lock the car door. Somebody might steal the Buick, and then they'd have to walk back to St. Louis, he said. Dad always thought thieves were lurking around, probably because on the Battleship Missouri somebody had swiped a pair of new socks his mother had mailed him. Those sock thieves were following Dad his whole life, even now in a hospital parking lot, ready to take the station wagon.

The waiting room was noisy, ammonia-smelling, and crowded with some old people who looked about ready to die. There were also a few young people who weren't too bad off—a crying boy with poison ivy and a girl with an ice bag on her wrist from falling off a skateboard. Elizabeth was whimpering the loudest and looked in so much pain, they got her in right away. Mom and Dad darted through the swinging doors of the emergency room with her. That left John, Patrick, and Teddy to watch baby Joey. A priest in black with his stiff white collar strolled past them toward the men's room, and Patrick remembered Mom had said to say a prayer.

He took a deep breath to think about how to begin. But then Teddy went over to the drinking fountain, and Patrick knew this was his chance. He hadn't been alone with John once since he had found out the secret of the ages just the night before. Baby Joey was on John's lap. It was quiet. Patrick began with a question, pretending he didn't know the answer.

"John?"

"Yeah."

"You ever wonder where babies come from?"

"What?"

"You ever wonder where babies come from?"

John looked at Patrick the way John Lennon looked at reporters during a press conference. "All you need is love," he said.

"What?"

Baby Joey started grunting out a turd in his diaper, and John handed him to Patrick.

"I wish I could tell you more, but I'm not supposed to."

Teddy came back, and Patrick tried to hand him baby Joey, but Teddy smelled the diaper.

"No way! You hold him."

John and Teddy got up and sat farther away from Patrick and baby Joey. Then some of the other patients got a whiff and also got up to sit farther away. That left Patrick alone with his baby brother in a row of empty chairs. Patrick looked at Joey's face. Did he even know how gross he was? His Gerber eyes were jolly and eager to make friends. If only Mom would come out with a Pamper. It was a bad one. Patrick fanned the air with a *Highlights* magazine and breathed through his mouth. That helped a little. But some of the air juices still worked their way into Patrick's nose. It was a long wait.

The priest came out of the men's room, tucking in his shirt. He walked over to the elevators and stabbed his finger at the Up button, and Patrick remembered he was supposed to pray. He tried to say a little prayer, starting out with how Elizabeth was always a good girl and how he hoped she could get better. But then his conscience accused him for wanting to go to the beach instead of the hospital, and for wanting to talk to John about where babies come from instead of praying, and for looking at the magazine at the gas station with the naked women in it, and for dropping the Wonder Bread bag full of pee on the highway. God didn't like it when Patrick tried to act holy in a crisis. He was onto him. Patrick looked at happy, stinky Joey and wished he could have prayed better to help Elizabeth, but he had nothing to bargain with. It was all up to the doctors.

Finally, after about a half hour, Mom and Dad came out with Elizabeth, and they said she was all right. The X-ray showed she was constipated.

"Patrick, are these yours?" Mom said, turning to Patrick like a prosecutor.

"What?"

She opened up her fist, and out blossomed a yellow wad of Juicy Fruit wrappers they had found in Elizabeth's pocket. There were about fifteen of them.

"Well, are they?"

She had him. Patrick had left his Jumbo pack on the dresser back at the cottage, and Elizabeth had swallowed the whole thing.

"I'm sorry."

"Sorry doesn't save lives," Dad said. "No more gum this trip for the whole family."

"What?" John and Teddy groaned. They looked at Patrick with disgust. Teddy was especially hard hit. Dad made the boys empty their pockets and turn over all their gum. Patrick lost the fresh, unopened pack of Juicy Fruit from Steiner's, and John and Teddy surrendered some Bazooka Joe. It was like one of those gangster movies where the police make the bootleggers empty all their whiskey barrels down the gutter, with men weeping on the sidelines. Dad took their gum and rifled it into the hospital trashcan. Other patients in the waiting room watched the whole thing.

"We need to wake up as a family," he said.

They drove back through the woods to the cottage. Nobody talked. No radio. No Pampers. The windows were down. Elizabeth sat in the front seat between Mom and Dad. John, Teddy, and Patrick sat holding their noses in the way back seat. And baby Joey—with a sculpture of warm, smashed poo between his butt cheeks—sat alone in the middle row, strapped in his car seat, asleep and peaceful.

# - chapter nine -

TAMMY AND GINNY looked beautiful in their swimsuits when Patrick first spotted them over by the State Park Pavilion. It wasn't easy finding them. First, he had to ditch Mom. He told her he needed to go over to the pavilion to use the bathroom. "Why don't you just go in the lake and pretend you're swimming?" she asked. That's what he usually did when he was playing Frisbee or snorkeling and didn't want to waste time walking up shore to use the bathroom. But today, he told Mom it wasn't right to pee in Lake Michigan.

"What if everybody did that? What would the beach smell like?"

"Patrick, I'm proud of you. You're maturing. You go ahead, but hurry right back."

"OK." He ran up shore, his bare feet splashing through the wet surf sand—weaving between little kids with plastic buckets and dads taking charge of sand castles. His own dad was back at the cottage waiting for the plumber to fix the leak and probably reading the *Antique Trader,* circling "interesting items" with a red pen while baby Joey and Elizabeth napped. Poor Dad. How boring. But Patrick was free, running like an escaped prisoner in the sun, naked except for his swimsuit. He didn't know yet how great the moment was. He wouldn't know until later in the year, when he was sitting at his school desk. That's when the nuns would have him. And the clock on the wall would mock him—*tick, tick, tick*—and the Number Two pencil in his grip would dig a groove in the sweaty bump on his middle finger as he wrote out columns of numbers and thought about how the skin between his toes itched but he wouldn't be able to take off his socks and shoes until after school.

Right now, though, he had the white surf fizzing like 7 Up bubbles across his ankles with the waves landing and pulling back. Lake air filled his lungs, as fresh as the air at the top of the Ferris wheel at the school picnic when they would stop to let somebody on, and he'd look down and see all the nuns and teachers who couldn't control his life for the whole summer sitting at their little table eating German potato salad. Looking at the lake, he could see the boys who were already wet and used to the water splashing their goose-bumpy, knee-deep moms who didn't want to get their hair wet. Teenaged guys with bikinied girlfriends on their shoulders waded out beyond the sandbar, toward the danger buoys where the water turned blue-green. Beyond that, way out, the lake was a deeper blue and silver-streaked with sun glare all the way to the horizon.

"I hope I never die," he whispered.

As he ran along, he passed an old man in a chair reading the book *The Love Machine* with his toes in the surf, then a pretty girl buried up to her neck by some handsome boys, and a few steps farther, a suntanned muscle man on his knees rubbing oil on his girlfriend's pointy shoulder blades. Patrick's eyes raced over bikini girls flying kites, bikini girls dripping wet, and bikini girls toweling off. There were bikini tops here and bikini bottoms there. It was a wild, sunlit, curvy crayon box of colors mixed together with the sound of everyone having fun. His ears blurred with laughter, flirty talk, and the tinny buzz of transistor radios playing the Beatles, Rolling Stones, and Elvis, all washed over by the whooshing of the surf. The beach was like a gazebo band at dusk with every musician practicing their own notes, on the verge of playing a new song Patrick's ears were thirsty to hear. Obviously, all these people knew the secret of the ages, which he could now see was the main reason humans throughout history had gone to the beach—to take off their clothes to swim together and think about getting a home run. He stopped to catch his breath and look around for Rex and the girls.

"Where are they?" he said, resting his hands on his knees.

Tammy and Ginny were out there somewhere. He stepped off the cool, wet surf sand onto the beach sand to navigate the maze between hundreds of beach towels. The beach sand was so hot, he started sprinting toward the pavilion. The Grand Haven postcards called it "singing sand," but really it was squeaking sand. *Squeak, squeak, squeak* with every dashing stride. Now he really *did* have to pee, so he ran like a comet for the pavilion. He ran so fast, he didn't see Rex and the girls. They saw him, and Rex hollered.

"Hey, Patrick! You idiot, over here."

His feet were on fire, so he just waved hello and ran into the State Park Pavilion. It was a long, one-story, blond brick building with a covered breezeway in the middle. The concrete floor was cool and sand-drifted. Tile walls ricocheted with shouts of little kids laughing and playing, and the chugging motor sound of the snow cone machine shaving ice. The breeze smelled of fresh salty popcorn, which no kid could eat without coming back for a large soda. Watching some younger boys spit their sodas at each other through straws, he envied them briefly for their obvious ignorance of the secret of the ages. Theirs was an afternoon free of the burden of having to kiss a girl. He looked away and entered the men's room. Older boys who had probably kissed lots of girls walked around with untanned, white bottoms and hairy front sides in the shower steam atmosphere. Patrick bellied up to the standup urinal and tried to go, but his bladder got bashful, just like at a Blues Hockey game when the score was tied and a long line of Teamsters would stand behind him burping and tapping their work boots. A naked teenager walked up next to him and started peeing right away like a garden hose. The teen had huge muscles galore and was bragging to another guy about how his GTO sports car had a stick shift. Patrick felt ashamed of his own wheels back home, a red Schwinn. It was nothing but a one-speed. Down hills it could outrun a poodle, but other boys had ten speeds that were fast. Finally he started peeing, but by the time he flushed, Patrick was losing confidence in himself and in the project Rex had planned. He felt like just a kid again.

"Where ya been?" Rex said, as he came out. Rex was waiting in the breezeway and looking at his hair in the reflection of the glass case displaying the Michigan state map. It was one of those *You-Are-Here* maps that Patrick always liked to study at rest stops to see how much farther they had to drive. Rex wanted to know why he was late, so Patrick told him.

"*Juicy Fruit?* Are you kidding me? I've been out here for an hour trying to keep from dying. Are you ready?"

"I don't know," Patrick said, facing the map with the highway leading back to St. Louis.

Rex punched him in the shoulder and told him to snap out of it. Patrick punched him back just as hard. They glared at each other.

"LOOK! Here's where we are," Rex said. "We've got one week, and Tammy and Ginny are right out there waiting for us." Rex wheeled Patrick's shoulders around facing the beach and pointed toward the girls. "All we have to do is go get them."

Patrick looked across the hot sand at Tammy and Ginny and then over at Rex. Rex was as zealous as Lawrence of Arabia planning to attack Aqaba. If Patrick said no, he would have to walk back to Mom and have a boring vacation. "OK, but what do we do?"

"Just go out there and talk nice. Tammy's mom and dad are there. He's a mean one. He's sitting in the best chair, chewing up a cigar and spitting out little pieces. He called you and me 'Yankee boys.'"

"Yankee boys?"

"I don't know what that means either. But Tammy's mom, now, she's more friendly. We have to fool them into letting us walk alone with the girls on the pier."

"OK."

Patrick gathered up his courage and followed Rex out across the scorching desert sand.

# - chapter ten -

A MAN WITH NO EYE LASHES, Tammy's dad, Mr. Jawthorne, looked ready to strike. His eyes reminded Patrick of a snake he had annoyed at the reptile house on a field trip to the zoo. Patrick had been tapping the glass—*tap, tap, tap, tap, tap*—then WHAM! The snake lunged and hit the glass sending all the kids, including Patrick, jumping back screaming. With high cheek bones and short, slicked-back hair, Mr. Jawthorne was coiled on a folding chair wearing white buckskin shoes, white pants, a white button-up shirt, and a blood-red tie. He sat with one leg crossed over the other at the knee, bobbing his shoe tensely. In the whole state of Michigan, there was no man so dressed up for the beach as Mr. Jawthorne.

Tammy and Ginny were stretched out on towels in their bikinis listening to a transistor radio with all their bare skin oiled up to catch the sun. Tammy's mom sat in the sand with her legs out, leaning into a canvas-back chair, reading a *Good Housekeeping* magazine. A woman with big black hair, she wore sassy sunglasses and a white, one-piece swimming suit decorated with green vines and pink flowers growing wildly across her big chest. She glanced up from her magazine and nodded hello. Patrick nodded back and looked over at Mr. Jawthorne. On the radio, Elvis Presley was singing "Suspicious Minds." Patrick stuck out his shaking hand, and Mr. Jawthorne grabbed it. He squeezed it long and tight, looking Patrick in the eyes, then let go.

"What choo boys want?" He took a slug from a bottle of Dr. Pepper dotted with condensation.

Patrick looked at Rex.

"Look at me, son."

"Sir?"

"What choo want comin' round courting these fresh, young girls?" He leaned to the side, keeping his eyes on Patrick, and spit a nub of his unlit cigar in the sand.

"Now, now, that's no way to begin," said Tammy's mother in a kind, *Good Housekeeping* voice. "It's such a lovely day."

"A might *too* lovely," he said, catching Patrick and Rex looking at the girls' oiled-up legs.

Ginny leaped up and came to the boys' defense. "Mr. Jawthorne, *puh-leez!* They's just coming by to go swimming and spend some time!"

The boys looked at Ginny standing there in her white bikini. She put one hand on her hip and the other on Patrick's shoulder. Her fingertips were tiny and soft. Watching all this from her towel, Tammy started laughing. She didn't care what happened to them.

"Set down, girl!" Mr. Jawthorne said to Ginny. "Your folks are trusting me to protect you this week like you was my own." He looked down at his daughter Tammy who had slipped her black bikini straps off her shoulders to baste on some more Johnson's Baby Oil. "Tammy! Get decent!"

"But Daddy!" Tammy whined.

"Do what he says," Tammy's mother whispered.

Tammy pushed her straps back up, and Ginny sat down next to her. Patrick and Rex stood still for the trial. Mr. Jawthorne swatted a sand fly off his shoe with his copy of his hunting magazine. "Boys," he said, "I. Know. Men. I run a trucking company with a hundred men working for me. And mind you it's not just a local concern. We run trucks all the way up north."

The boys nodded. Patrick wondered if any of his truckers were putting quarters in those machines they have in the gas station by Abraham Lincoln's house.

"By the way, what state you from?"

"Missouri," Rex said.

"Missouri? Hmmmm," he said, twisting his ear lobe, considering the entire Missouri map and its role in Civil War history. One hundred years earlier, Mr. Jawthorne's family had lost lives, property, and great wealth in the Civil War. At family gatherings ever since, with wet, chewed-up cigars chomped between their teeth, the Jawthorne men recounted bitterly how their mansion outside

Atlanta had been burned by Union devils. Only now, through his trucking company, was Mr. Jawthorne climbing back up to the foothills of the mountain from which his ancestors had been pushed. "What part of Missouri?"

"St. Louis," Patrick said.

"St. Louis?" he leaned back, confused. St. Louis had Union and Southern sympathizers. "Well, what side was you on?"

Tammy's mother slapped her *Good Housekeeping* on her thighs and raised her voice. "Oh, let's not start that now!"

"Not startin' nothin'," Mr. Jawthorne said, getting louder, "just want to know what side."

"What side?" Patrick asked.

"In the war!" Mr. Jawthorne said, leaning forward.

"The battleship Missouri."

"No, no, no … not *that* war, I mean the *waruh*."

Patrick and Rex looked at each other and shrugged. Tammy's mother opened her magazine and flipped through the pages fast looking for a Jell-O recipe or something pleasant. Just then, Ginny sat up, eyes toward the lake.

"Look!"

They all looked. It was a big cargo ship, longer than a football field, as tall as a sand dune in the Arabian Desert, and pointed straight toward the pier.

"Why, it's beautiful, just like a dream ship," Tammy's mother said, her voice full of that maiden's melody that had won her husband many years ago. "There must be young couples on their honeymoon who've been dancing and watching the moon last night while they crossed the lake … in love."

"It's coming in the harbor!" Rex said. "If we hurry, we can run out there and watch it come in."

Ginny jumped up, yawning. "Can we go, Mr. Jawthorne?"

"No. We don't need to go chasing after some love boat."

"But it's a cargo ship," Rex said.

"Oh, let them go have a little fun," Tammy's mother said, rubbing her husband's knee. Her touch was calming and hinted at all the womanly ways she possessed to pull the bad electricity out of him.

He looked at her tan hand on his white pants and softened. "Well, maybe it wouldn't be so bad as long as it's a cargo ship."

Tammy sat up and saw the black smoke coming out the stacks.

"Oh, Daddy, I remembered what it was I wanted to tell you."

"What?"

Tammy's southern accent plinked out the words as sweet as upper notes on a piano. She pointed at Patrick. "Today at the drugstore, that one said something about Sherman burning Atlanta."

"WHAT?!!!" Mr. Jawthorne rose to his feet. His Dr. Pepper fell over and spilled in the sand like a volcano in the school science fair. "SHERMAN?!" he roared.

Patrick and Rex started to back off. Mr. Jawthorne took a step toward Patrick, rolling up his hunting magazine like a sword. "You makin' sport of us with your Sherman talk?"

"Why, no, sir, I just—"

"Jus' *what?*"

"We have to go, see you girls later," Rex said running off.

Patrick stood watching Mr. Jawthorne's eyes boiling and his white pants legs striding toward him.

"You'd better go," Tammy's mother said.

Ginny looked at Patrick sadly, shaking her head. Tammy just smiled. Patrick bolted off after Rex, who was running toward the pier.

"And don't choo come around here after these girls again!" Mr. Jawthorne yelled in their wake.

# - chapter eleven -

THEY RAN HARD without stopping until they got up on the south pier. The cargo ship cut slowly through the channel between the north and south pier. It stretched six hundred feet long from the fog house to the lighthouse—a massive magic trick of metal afloat. High up near the bow, blue-green water shot out of a hole to lighten the ship so it wouldn't scrape bottom. The boys waved to some deckhands, and they waved back. Rex told Patrick the deckhands would go into port to unload boxes and then probably go ashore to meet some girls and get home runs. And he didn't just tell him; Rex said it with a heaving sigh of lament for their own lack of progress with Tammy and Ginny.

The cargo ship surged up the Grand River, churning brown water astern. Its horn let off a deep, sad note while the boys walked along thinking. Patrick saw a bloated fish floating on its side in the river and felt sorry for him, his gills opening and closing in a silent prayer to get back out in the lake. On the lakeside, the blue water stretched all the way down to Holland, many miles south where the point was blurry with fog. The Grand Haven beach they had just run from looked as far away as a dream after breakfast, but still sandy bright, sprinkled with people in bathing suits around the pavilion, and behind that, the State Park lot was lined with silver streamliner campers, and farther inland, the dunes rose up with clumps of forest and cottages whose picture windows kept constant vigil on the fickle face of the lake.

"Ginny likes you," Rex said.

"Yeah, right."

"No, really. I can tell."

A wave splashed against the sitting ledge then foamed across the winter-pocked walkway, about thirty-five feet wide, to the Grand River side of the pier. They skittered and ran barefoot, dodging the cold water and uneven concrete seams that could gash a toe bloody. Every few steps they had to duck under the black iron struts supporting the catwalk that ran down the center of the pier. The catwalk legs were sticky with spider webs here and there, spun up to the wooden plank walkway where the lighthouse man could run during storms to avoid giant waves.

"Can't you see what's hidden just below the surface?" Rex lectured Patrick.

Rex was convinced that Ginny wanted to kiss Patrick, out of pity, and that Tammy would kiss anybody just to feel one moment's freedom from her father. "It's hopeless," Patrick said. "We should just go fishing this week." He sat down on the concrete ledge by the lighthouse. Rex was deep in thought and preparing his next move like a chess master. Couples holding hands walked along past the fishermen who lined the pier on the lakeside. Love graffiti decorated the red lighthouse—"Bob loves Jan," and "Clank + Nina." The boys struck up a conversation with an old man fishing. A widower with diabetes, he had a double chin and an hour-long stare, watching his line.

"Any luck?"

"Not for a while."

With a scratchy voice, he told the boys that the perch of late July were running in toward the pier last week. Thousands of them had been caught. But then last night's thunderstorm charged in from the lake.

"That lighting scared the shit out of them," he said. "It hit the water like arc welding, and they went back out deep."

They sat there and watched a speedboat pulling a teenaged guy on water skis skipping across the water.

"You ever do that?" Patrick asked the man.

"Yeah, but not anymore. Them days are gone."

He tightened his line, and a blonde girl in a bikini passed by walking a dog. All three of them, old man and young boys, looked over and watched her bikini bottom walking away.

"Them days are gone too."

Rex jabbed Patrick hard and pointed at the girl.

"It's her!"

"Who?"

It was the girl from Indiana. She had walked right past them. They didn't recognize her without binoculars. Rex shot up and followed her. The fisherman looked at Patrick.

"You'd better go, too, while you can." Right then, he got a bite and turned away to set the hook. Patrick got up and ran after Rex.

"Rex, I can't be gone this long. My mom thinks I'm going to the bathroom."

"Shhhhh … so, tell her you had diarrhea. Come on."

They spy-walked about fifty feet behind her, pretending they were going out to the end of the pier like everyone else. Her little dog was on a leash, sniffing the base of the catwalk struts where they were bolted to the pier blocks. Whenever the dog stopped, the boys stopped, pretending to study the lake or cobwebs on the catwalk. Her bikini was lemon yellow, and the bra top made a smile shape across her suntanned chest. When she turned the corner at the end of the pier, they could see her yellow-covered breasts outlined against the blue water.

"She's perfect," Rex said.

"She looks a little sad."

"Sad? Are you kidding? How can you look at *that* and see sad? Come on."

To Patrick, though, she did look sad. Maybe it was the way she walked a little slow and disappointed, or kept her head down now and then, or the way the muscles around her eyes squinted, as if she felt something nobody else on the pier could feel, not even her dog, and she was carrying that feeling all by herself. Patrick wished he was older, the kind of boy who could just walk up to sad girls and say the right joke and make them smile and want to kiss him.

"You should go talk to her," Rex said.

"Talk to her? I don't know what to say."

"I know ... I know … Maybe, pretend we're lost ... That's it, ask her for directions."

"Directions? You can't ask for directions on a pier. There's only one way off."

"Well, just tell her you're from out of town, and *then* ask for directions."

They went back and forth arguing until they lost sight of her behind the fog house on the very end of the pier. Then they hurried around the lakeside of the fog house, where the green scum puddles were slippery, and arrived at the end of the pier. It was a solemn spot where big pole fishermen and boat watchers and splash catchers share a few moments together on the brink of the lake, then go separate ways and never get together again their whole life. They spotted her standing on the Grand River side talking to a couple of older guys by the fog house. They were suntanned guys, the kind that hang around the pavilion men's room with muscles everywhere and muscle cars parked outside. Patrick thought they acted like they knew her, or maybe they acted that way because they were teenagers and had talked to lots of girls. Rex and Patrick whistled past the three of them and overheard her saying, "Maybe," as if they were asking her for a date.

"My mom is going to kill me," Patrick said. "I've been gone way too long." Rex agreed to break off the spying and get back to the shore. On the way back, on the pier, they saw Patrick's brother John walking toward them. He was holding hands with a cute redhead in a blue bikini. Patrick stared at John and caught his eyes as they passed, but John acted like John Lennon leaving a concert with a lot on his mind.

"Isn't that your brother?" Rex said.

"Yeah."

"*He* knows how to meet girls."

Patrick and Rex jogged down the beach past the pavilion back to where Mom was waiting. She stood up, big and pregnant, with both hands on her hips, when she saw Patrick.

"Where have you been, young man? I sent John out to find you. Did you see John?"

"No."

"Now *he's* missing. What took you so long?

"Oh, he had diarrhea," Rex said.

# - chapter twelve -

REX WAS RIGHT about the girls. Tammy and Ginny were ready to meet up with them that very night. Patrick and his family were in the cottage after dinner, a little before sunset, when Rex knocked on the kitchen door. Mom let him in. "Why, Rex, what are you doing out by yourself? Do your parents know you're roaming about? It's almost dark." On like that she went in a sing-songy voice. That was her way of saying, *Shouldn't you go home?*

But Rex didn't pay any attention. "Oh, I'm fine. The folks are watching TV about the moon launch."

"That's right; the launch is tomorrow," Dad called out. He was in the knotty-pine dining room, working on a model car with Teddy while John was sculpting his modeling clay into the head of Jesus. John couldn't think of anything to make, so Mom told him to sculpt Jesus. The whole family was busy. Elizabeth was drawing with crayons in a new coloring book, and baby Joey was crawling around the rug, putting lost destroyers from the game Battleship in his mouth. Patrick was the only one who didn't have a project, so he was glad to see Rex and hoped for good news.

"Patrick, can you bust up this bag of ice for me?" Mom said.

"Sure." He picked up a twenty-pound plastic bag of ice to drop on the kitchen floor.

"Not here; go outside on the concrete," she said.

Rex followed him out where it was private. It was a fine twilight with somebody's barbecue smoke in the breeze and the pavement still giving off warmth from the heat of the day. Patrick hugged the bag of ice cubes as he walked. The cold went right through his shirt and felt good on his sunburn.

"It's all set. They're going to meet us at the lookout at sunset."

"Really?" Patrick was so excited he dropped the bag of ice half on his foot.

Rex shook his head at Patrick's bad aim, but kept going. "I caught up with them over at the Khardomah Lodge. They were playing pinball. And they had a big laugh about everything today, and I asked them to meet us at sunset at the lookout. *Sunset!* You know what that means."

"Sunset!" Patrick said picking up the ice. *"Love American Style!"* All the cubes were loose in the bag now but still freezing against his chest. "What about Mr. Jawthorne?"

"He's probably watching the moon stuff, too, him and his wife. He won't bother us."

"I don't know if I can sneak away. We're having a family night."

Rex took a step back. "*Family night?* Ginny is your family tonight. She's probably putting on fresh ChapStick right now. She feels sorry for you."

"Sorry?"

"For getting yelled at by Mr. Jawthorne."

They went inside, and Patrick gave the smashed-up ice bag to Mom. She ripped it open and poured it into the cooler, clinking across a row of coke bottles.

"Mom," Patrick said softly so Dad wouldn't hear, "do you think Rex and me can go and watch the sunset?"

"Rex and *I*," she said as loud as a teacher. "It's not Rex and *me*. It's Rex and I."

"Rex and I. Do you think we can?"

"Can what?" Dad called out from the model kit table.

Patrick took a breath to make something up.

"He wants to go out alone with Rex by the lookout," Mom told Dad.

"I don't think so. Not tonight, Patrick," Dad said as his thumb left a glue print on the model car windshield. "It's almost time to go into town and watch the Musical Fountain."

"Dad! You just ruined the windshield!" Teddy whined.

"We'll fix it," Dad said.

Rex kicked Patrick, and he cleared his throat to argue for early parole.

"Dad, I hate the Musical Fountain. Rex and me—"

"Rex and I," Mom interrupted.

"Rex and I—"

"No, I'm sorry; we need to stick together as a family this trip so there aren't any problems," Dad said. "This is a family vacation."

Rex sighed.

"Please, Dad," Patrick said softly, "I won't get in any trouble."

Dad looked at him and thought about it. Patrick hadn't gotten in any real trouble with the police for a long time. "Well, I guess it wouldn't hurt. What do you think?" he asked Mom.

"Patrick, I'm sorry, but I want you to take it easy tonight after your diarrhea."

"Diarrhea?" Dad said. He perked up, because Dad ate All Bran cereal before going downtown every day and was always interested in proper bowel movements. "Oh, I didn't know about that. You'd better stick with the family in case you need to go to the bathroom."

Patrick hung his head low.

"Patrick, there'll be other sunsets," Mom said.

"Not like tonight," he said.

Rex gave up. "All right, Patrick, I'll see you tomorrow."

"Well, not tomorrow, Rex," Dad called out. "We're going on a little jaunt. You'll have to wait until Wednesday."

"Wednesday? I thought we're just going on a short ride in the morning," Patrick said.

"Oh, no," Mom said. "It's Greenfield Village over by Detroit. Have your parents ever taken you to Greenfield Village, Rex?"

"No, my dad just golfs, and my mom shops." Rex was getting disgusted with Patrick's family.

"It's terrific," Dad called out. "They've got the Henry Ford Museum. It's history."

"See you, Patrick."

"See you."

Rex left dejected, and everyone but Patrick went back to their projects. John sculpted the face of Jesus. Teddy tried to rub Dad's glue thumbprint off the model car windshield. Elizabeth colored a giraffe yellow, and baby Joey found a stray CHEEZ-IT on the rug and put it in his mouth. Patrick opened the freezer to hide his face so no one could see he was so mad he was about to cry. Cold freezer air poofed out as the eyes of the dead fish on the stringer stared back at him.

"Shut the freezer door, Patrick," Mom said. "Maybe we'll get some ice cream at the Dairy Treat before the Musical Fountain."

The mention of ice cream set off a roar of excitement from all the other kids. Everyone put down their paintbrushes and model kit and crayons, and off they went in the station wagon to downtown Grand Haven. Patrick was so angry he cussed his parents under his breath. Dark, secret cuss words formed in his mouth. Cuss words he had heard an appliance repairman say a long time ago and never planned to say himself. But now, they danced on his tongue like flames scorching a marshmallow over a roaring campfire. This family had him trapped. Dad saw Patrick was sad and kidded around with him when he bought him an ice cream cone under the orange lights at the Dairy Treat walkup window. Dad tricked Patrick into smiling a little. But then that made him even more disgusted that Dad was able to control his life by interrupting the bad mood he wanted to hold onto.

"Let's go see the Musical Fountain and have a good time," Mom said.

They walked along the sidewalk licking their cones with Mom pushing baby Joey in the stroller and everybody forced to hold hands at the crosswalks. It was a terrible feeling. Then Patrick looked up the street and saw the bright lights of the Grand Theatre marquee and noticed the row of motorcycles parked on the street. The sign said the movie was *Easy Rider*.

"Hey, John, look!" Patrick said.

"Cool, I want to see that movie before we go home."

"Oh, no," Mom said right away. Dad read the marquee and announced that not all movies are good for the family. Patrick and John exchanged glances, each thinking the exact same thing: a family can really wreck your family vacation.

The Musical Fountain started at sunset with a lighted geyser shooting up on Dewey Hill, the sand dune across the harbor. From loud speakers, a voice as calm as a funeral home director said, "Good evening and welcome … I am the Grand Haven Musical Fountain." Hundreds of families with ice cream on their lips and sugar surging through their veins sat on bleachers as pleasure boats sputtered into harbor, cutting their engines and dropping anchors. The air was sticky and still, smelling of sunburn lotion, far away cigarettes, and bug spray. Throughout the crowd, moms were shaking cans of OFF, making babies cry as the cold spray on their arms and legs startled them from stroller naps. Baby Joey fussed and ended up in Patrick's lap. The funeral home voice introduced a list of songs only old people liked—the music from *South Pacific*. The syrupy songs played while the water from twenty fountains danced in waves and surges of ever-changing colored lights. Mosquitos moved in like Japanese Zeroes over Pearl Harbor, and Patrick sat there between Mom and Dad watching people in front of them slap at their necks. All Patrick could think of was how Rex must be on the lookout RIGHT NOW sitting between Tammy and Ginny, catching the cool, lake breeze. The stars were coming out. Rex, Tammy, and Ginny had probably seen the big orange sun melt into the lake without him. Now Rex was probably sitting between them so tight he could feel their side arms touching his, their skin as cool as fresh bed sheets. But Rex couldn't kiss *both* of them, so nothing was happening. Except maybe they were laughing at Patrick for being in such an awful family and walking around drug stores carrying a canister of itchy bottom powder.

# - chapter thirteen -

THE APOLLO ELEVEN ASTRONAUTS suited up to blast off for the moon while Patrick's family stumbled in the dark to get in the station wagon for the three-hour drive to the Henry Ford Museum near Detroit. Patrick was so tired he didn't remember the first part of the trip. Everybody but Dad, who was driving, took a nap. Then around nine thirty, Dad turned on the radio loud and told everybody to listen up. The news announcer described how the tall lunar rocket shot out smoke and white-hot flames and lifted off slowly from Cape Kennedy as thousands of people watched and cheered, standing on car hoods, atop campers, or beside tents.

"This is history," Dad said. "You should remember this all your life. We're going to the moon!"

Everyone was quiet.

"I thought we were going to Deh-toit," Elizabeth said.

The family laughed at her, even Mom and Dad. Then Elizabeth buried her head in her pillow to cry, and Dad snapped his fingers and told everyone to not make fun of her anymore.

"You're the only girl we have, and we love you very much," Dad said, reaching back and patting her shoulder.

Mom reached around, too, and said she had a surprise for Elizabeth that she brought along in case the trip got boring. Elizabeth perked up, and Mom gave her a doll that wets her pants.

"It's Betsy Wetsy," Mom said handing it to her in the package. "Someday you'll grow up and have a real baby that wets her pants."

Dad looked in the rearview mirror. "What? Does that thing really wet? What about the upholstery?"

"Oh, don't worry, it'll be all right," Mom said.

Elizabeth got out Betsy Wetsy and held her as Dad said not to put any water in her until the car trip was over. John whispered to Patrick that they should put some Coca-Cola in her and see what happens. But they didn't get a chance that morning. Before the astronauts were a half hour in space, the family pulled into Greenfield Village.

"Everyone stick together," Dad said, "and be sure to lock the car." He popped a downtown breath mint in his mouth and led the way.

The sun was up over the trees now, and the day was getting warm. Patrick tried not to think of the good times he was missing on the beach with Rex and Tammy and Ginny. Before him was an amusement park of American history, a make-believe town that millionaire Henry Ford had built to display all the wonders of progress. Ford had an exhibit hall full of antique cars, a hangar lined with airplanes, and another with rows of historic trains. Visitors walked from building to building to see all that America had wrought. Mom had Joey in the baby stroller with Elizabeth at her side while John, Patrick, and Teddy roamed in short bursts toward anything interesting—as long as they kept Mom and Dad in sight.

"Don't get lost," Dad warned.

There was a little shack called Thomas Edison's workshop. It had a talking, rubber dummy of Thomas Edison standing behind a table with an array of beakers and secret equipment. Edison talked about how he set his goal of making the sixty-watt light bulb and never gave up, even though it was hard. The three-click reading lamp Dad had at home by his chair came later. Edison's last breath from when he died was on display in a corked beaker. Patrick asked the guide if they ever opened it up, just to smell it, and he said no. Another building had two actors, one pretending to be Abraham Lincoln, and the other a man named Douglas. They were arguing over abolition, and Lincoln got worked up, swinging his arms and raising his voice. Patrick felt sorry for Lincoln, because his beard kept shifting when he got excited. In another building, they had the rocking chair Lincoln was in when he was shot. That room was quiet and people filed past the chair in silent reverence.

The family then took a ride on a white, gingerbread-trimmed steamboat called the Suwannee. It paddled around a doughnut-shaped lagoon with the whistle blowing for about fifteen minutes, then let them off where they started. John, Patrick, and Teddy ran to the top deck and leaned over the railing to see the whole village and spit into the water. Teddy missed, and his spit dotted the bare arm of a man on the lower deck who looked up at them and got furious. They ran back down to hide from him and stayed with Mom and Dad until the ride ended.

"This is fabulous!" Dad said over and over again as Mom just nodded and pushed the stroller along under the hot sun with the baby in her belly sloshing around and kicking her in the ribs.

It was a lot of walking, through tree-lined streets with houses where famous people were born. Henry Ford had so much money he paid to have their houses moved there to show them off. They had the house where the Wright brothers were born, and another house where Noah Webster invented his dictionary. Patrick and John tried to look up the word "airplane" in an old dictionary they had there. But it wasn't even listed yet.

"Just think," the guide said, "sixty-five years ago, Wilbur and Orville took their first flight. And today we're going for the moon."

A brass band played Sousa songs from a front porch as they walked by. People dressed like pioneers boiled soap in a kettle, and visitors fed goats with a baby bottle. There was something to see at every turn—a big windmill from Cape Cod, a covered bridge from Pennsylvania, and an old fire engine house from New Hampshire. And then the family had a fried chicken lunch at a place on the grounds called the Clinton Inn, which Mom said was too expensive.

"We need to live it up and make every moment count this trip," Dad argued.

After lunch, Mom and Patrick were sitting on a park bench with baby Joey while Dad was off with the rest of the family at the blacksmith shop. This was Mom's chance to talk to Patrick about something bothering her. She hadn't been very involved with her older boys lately because of baby Joey and the new baby on the way, and she felt she needed to show Patrick some moral guidance. That sort of thing was easy in past years, when she only had a few kids at home and time to make Tollhouse cookies after school and talk with the kids. Now, she was in the endless Illinois cornfields of her life journey, miles and miles away from the younger mom she had once been. And her older boys were reaching toward the shiny and tempting things of adolescence, while the little ones still needed hands held and diapers changed. And to make things worse, another labor and delivery was fast approaching. Labor was the one load no one else could share, and she dreaded it. It was a kind of surrendering to be shot at dawn that only other women could understand. The thought of the pain and the pushing loomed over the summer vacation like a thunderstorm rushing off the lake, the kind that makes swimmers run for the shore, grabbing their towels to abandon the beach. No wonder she had been so short and fussy with everyone.

"Patrick, do you know where babies come from?"

The steamboat whistle blew. He was bee stung by the question. Did John tell her he had been asking questions? Or had Dad told her about the "S" volume encyclopedia at Rex's cottage? He didn't know whom to blame. Silent and embarrassed, he rubbed his nose and shrugged.

"You'll be going into fifth grade this fall," she said, "You're growing up."

"Yeah."

"I just want you to know. If you ever have any questions about life, about things like this, you should get your answers from your dad and me, *not other boys*. That's the way God wants it. God is watching over you."

There it was. She was bringing out her big battleship. God was watching him. Patrick looked around for some escape. But she kept talking about how God had put her and Dad in charge of his life to keep him right, and how he shouldn't try to find any answers from boys like Rex. They might tell him wrong things. Patrick knew this wasn't true, because Rex was the only one who cared enough to tell him the truth.

"Can I go to the blacksmith shop now?'

"Did you hear what I said?"

"Yeah."

"OK, you can go."

He ran fast and mad around the corner to the blacksmith shop and caught up with the rest of the family as they watched the blacksmith pound an orange, hot, glowing rod with a hammer. But Patrick kept his distance, too angry to stand near anyone in his family. The blacksmith pounded. The rod pinged. Sparks flew. That's exactly how he felt. Through his own research, by spending the night at Rex's, he had discovered the secret truth of where babies come from—a truth that parents everywhere kept hidden from kids, and now Mom was trying to pound him with the hammer of parenthood into the kind of boy she wanted him to become with no regard for what he wanted. God was behind all this. God was using his parents to work against him. And God probably was working against him to keep him from kissing Ginny before the trip was over. But he wasn't going to let God ruin his vacation. He looked at the blacksmith, and the blacksmith looked up at him. Patrick gave him a mean look, and the blacksmith pulled back his hammer and hurled his blows all the harder. Right then and there, Patrick resolved he was going to get back to Grand Haven and kiss Ginny on her ChapStick-slathered lips no matter what God, his parents, or anybody else wanted. After all, that was the message of Greenfield Village. No one can do great things if he gives up. No one can invent the light bulb or take off for the moon by quitting. And no one can kiss a girl if he doesn't try, try, try. The blacksmith pounded that rod then dunked it in a barrel of cold, hissing water and held it up for everyone to see. He looked back up at Patrick like it was a challenge, like he was saying, "I hammered this rod straight, what are you going to do?"

# - chapter fourteen -

NIGHT HAD FALLEN, and the family station wagon hurtled under a billion stars down a dark interstate surrounded by farm country. Content and drowsy after hamburgers and malts at Burger Chef, everyone was quiet—listening to the lullaby of the Buick pistons and feeling the cool night air slip through the open windows, soothing their sunburned faces. Patrick chewed on a Burger Chef napkin, and then, pretending he was a Zulu Warrior hunting rhino with a blow dart, fired spit wads through his straw from the way back seat all the way to Dad's rearview mirror. The deadly projectiles landed with a *THWAMP*.

Sitting next to Patrick, John got in on it, too. It was a relaxing retreat into immaturity without words. Words were something Patrick was avoiding with John. He wished he could tell his older brother about the bet to kiss a girl, and how he knew about baseball. Maybe get some advice. But Patrick was afraid Mom could be getting information out of John. So he kept quiet as they rode along, thinking about Ginny's lips and how he might tilt his head like in the movies and kiss her.

Dad kept driving down the highway, not noticing all the spit wads piling up on the rearview mirror. There were about fifteen of them. Then the boys saw his eyes looking in the mirror, and his free hand grabbed one of the spit wads. He held it up to Mom.

"Honey, what are these?"

"I don't know, probably the boys."

That's when the trouble began. Dad switched on the overhead light and looked around. Patrick and John ducked out of sight. Dad whispered to Mom something urgent they couldn't hear. John and Patrick peeked up over the seat back. Mom was turned around looking for something. Then she said it.

*"Where's Elizabeth?"*

"Hey, John, Patrick!" Dad called out. "Have you got Elizabeth back there?"

"No," they said in unison. They looked over into the middle seat. Teddy and baby Joey were there, but Elizabeth's seat was empty, except for her Betsy Wetsy doll lying on its side.

*"Oh, dear God!"* Mom cried. *"Dear God!"*

They had left her at the Burger Chef and driven fifty miles into the night.

Dad switched off the overhead light and stepped on the gas. The engine roared. Usually Dad went the speed limit, but even in the way back, John and Patrick knew he'd blown past that. They craned their necks to read the speedometer—*over a hundred miles an hour!* The Buick wagon was like Apollo Eleven burning past barns and empty fields.

"Everybody say a prayer," Mom told them, her voice cracking.

John and Patrick slumped in their seats. Patrick looked out the back window and saw the Michigan night with the stars pulling back over the fields. Elizabeth was out there somewhere. Probably crying, all alone. He felt awful for her. Turning his head to the side so John wouldn't see, he started praying.

"Dear God," he thought. But nothing else would come. His conscience was accusing him. He'd said too many cuss words the night before and had been too mad at God all afternoon to pray right now when he needed to. He had been thinking too much about kissing Ginny and first base and home runs. All he could pray was to say her name. "Elizabeth." He tried to get God to think about *her* and not about him, but the only thing he could think to say sounded fake. "If she's okay," he prayed in his mind, "I'll help out more with the dishes." The loud whine of the tires on the road told him that wasn't enough. So, with nobody hearing, he started again, reluctantly.

"If she's OK, I won't kiss Ginny."

Dad passed a big truck and got off at the next exit. He zoomed into a State Police Headquarters, which he had learned about from a sign back on the highway. The car screeched to a stop, and Mom and Dad threw open their doors. "Lock the doors and don't anybody move!" Dad hollered as he followed Mom, already rushing toward the building.

The four boys sat there dead quiet. Baby Joey was sleeping. He was the only one who got through the crisis relaxed. Finally, after about five minutes, Dad and Mom came out looking better.

"She's OK," Dad said. "The police have her in Grand Rapids." He put his hand on Mom's shoulder and squeezed. Mom nodded and wiped her eyes.

When they got to the Grand Rapid police station, it was the same thing. Dad and Mom went in and told the kids to lock the doors and don't talk to strangers and stay put. This time they all watched for her. She came out the police door under the streetlight, and the boys all cheered. Elizabeth climbed in and grabbed her Betsy Wetsy as Mom buckled her in tight.

Then Dad shut the door and gave a stern lecture.

"We have got to wake up as a family. From now on, whenever we go anywhere, I want you all to count off from oldest to youngest. And we'll never leave until everyone's safe and accounted for."

So they counted off.

"One," John said.

"Two," Patrick said,

"Three," Teddy said.

Mom told Elizabeth to say "four," but she was too stunned from it all. So Mom said "four" for her.

"I'll say 'five' for Joey," Dad said.

Dad steered the Buick back onto the highway and they headed toward the lake and the waiting cottage in silence.

# - chapter fifteen -

PATRICK ALWAYS FELT SORRY for the Pharaoh of ancient Egypt. In religion class, the other boys liked Moses because he could make things happen. Blood in the river, dead fish, frogs, gnats, hailstones—Moses called down one plague after another—and each time, Pharaoh would admit the bad he had done and promise to do good. Then Moses would swing his stick and make the plague stop. But after the trouble was over, Pharaoh would go back to his old ways. Sister Hilga, a short nun with thick arms who carried in a big TV so the class could watch the 1968 World Series with the Cardinals and the Tigers, had warned the kids there's a Pharaoh lurking in every human heart. That's nun talk, Patrick knew, but he thought of the Pharaoh the next morning when he heard an engine revving outside the cottage and looked down from his bedroom window to see Rex sitting on a minibike. *A minibike!* Patrick ran down the steps and outside. The sun was shining. The lake was blue. He forgot all about the plagues of yesterday and remembered the lure of Ginny's lips.

"WHAT ARE YOU DOING?" Patrick shouted over the engine, which Rex kept on revving with a show-off grin.

"Get on."

Patrick stopped to think. His parents and everybody but Teddy had gone to Meijer's to get more groceries. Teddy came out, too, and took in the scene. Patrick knew he couldn't just get on and leave, because Teddy would tell Mom and Dad. And Dad had always told them to never ride a motorcycle, which is what a minibike is. It was right up there with cigarettes and tattoos to Dad.

"HAVE YOU GOT ANY GUM?" Patrick shouted. He could see Rex was chomping on a big wad.

"What?" He eased back on the engine.

"Give me a piece of gum."

Rex gave Patrick a stick of Teaberry cinnamon gum, and Patrick gave it to Teddy, but made him promise first not to tell Mom and Dad about the minibike. "Just tell them I went to play with Rex, but leave out the part about the bike."

"OK."

Teddy put the gum in his mouth, blinked at the cinnamon sting, and looked happy with the deal. No one in the family had tasted gum since Monday, when Dad threw all their gum in the trash. Patrick got on the black leather seat with barely any room to fit. It was just a one-boy minibike. And Rex told him to "hang on for his life." Grabbing Rex around the waist, Patrick felt the wind in his face as they ripped down the hill with the blue lake on his left and the hillside of cottages on his right. Rex went full throttle, and they got the minibike up to twenty-two miles an hour. His mother had told Rex to stay on the sidewalk, but when no cars were coming, he got out in the street. They sped past the State Park beach with all its silver campers and the pavilion, past the pier with the red lighthouse, and around the corner hugging the Grand River until they came to the A&W Root Beer stand at the bottom of the big sand dune. They pulled in and got off.

"Big things are happening," Rex said.

"What?"

"Let's get some root beer first."

They went up to the window and waited in line behind a motorcycle man. He was ordering the Papa burger, the Mama burger, and fries and root beers. It felt good to be in a motorcycle gang for a change, instead of always being in a station wagon. There were motorcycles roaring all over town for that movie *Easy Rider*. Patrick looked over at Rex's bike parked there in the sun.

"Where'd you get the bike?"

"Rented it. Well, my Mom rented it, because I was so bored yesterday when you weren't around. The girls were gone, too. They all went to the Dutch Village."

"The Dutch Village?"

"You know, back by the highway with the giant wooden shoe?"

"Oh, yeah, I saw that. What's is it?"

"You know, carnival rides, fudge, and guys making wooden shoes."

"Boring."

"Yeah, I know. How was your trip?"

"Boring … lots of history. One good part—we went on a steamboat and my brother spit on a man's arm down below."

"Cool. Did he chase you?"

"No."

"That's too bad."

It was their turn, and Rex ordered a couple of root beers. The lady served them in big frosty mugs, not the little kiddie mugs Patrick used to get at A&W with his parents. Rex didn't have any money, so the lady looked at Patrick, and he had to bust up a five-dollar bill hidden in a secret slot of his wallet since spring. Dad had given it to him for getting his grades up from D's and C's to mostly B's.

"I've got a plan," Rex said as they sat down at one of the picnic tables in the open air where everybody ate at A&W. Patrick scraped the frost off the side of the mug with his thumbnail and listened. Rex talked about how with the minibike they could take Ginny and Tammy for rides with the girls hanging and on tight.

"So?"

"Don't you see? That will get them used to feeling close to us, so they'll *want* to kiss us."

"I doubt it."

"No, it's true. I've studied it. You take these motorcycle gangs."

"Yeah?"

"They've got girls riding on the backs of their motorcycles all the time, so they must have lots of home runs, and why?"

"I don't know."

"Because the girls are so used to hanging on to keep from getting their head cracked open on the highway."

Rex made it sound right, even though they couldn't go out on the highway with the minibike and the top speed was around twenty-two miles an hour. They toasted it and laughed. While Patrick was laughing, he remembered how John and he had laughed so hard after they got away from the biker gang on the highway. So Patrick bragged and told Rex the whole Wonder Bread bag story. Rex thought it was the best thing Patrick had ever accomplished, and he smacked the table laughing.

"You showed those bikers! Hah!" Rex said.

They were finishing off their root beers, when somebody gave off a long, rumbling root beer burp right behind them. It was the biker who had ordered the Papa burger. They looked around and saw him standing over them.

"Wonder Bread bag?" he said.

It was the Viking, the lead biker from the pee bomb incident. Patrick noticed his long hair and red beard, then looking over at the table behind them, he saw the biker's girlfriend, the woman with long, braided hair running down her back It was them, all right.

"Somebody I want you to meet."

"Oh, we have to go," Rex said.

"That's right. I have to help at home with the dishes," Patrick added.

"Dishes can wait." They got up, and the Viking led them with a tight grip on their necks over to the back of the A&W, right at the bottom of the sand dune. His girlfriend followed. There were six motorcycles parked and the rest of the gang standing around sharing a cigarette. It was a hippie vacation, a group of escape artists on the road, fleeing the future and the past into the asphalt bosom of the present; dirty men with beards and whiskers, cruddy-looking jeans, fat belt buckles, scuffed-up boots, and nothing to look forward to but tree-trimming jobs, odd factory work, and house painting. The two women had faces as suntanned as catcher's mitts. The Viking's girlfriend was a former state highway worker who had just quit her job holding a SLOW sign. The other was a frizzy-haired waitress who skipped a shift to go on the trip, not knowing if she would have a job when she got back. Patrick could smell their B.O. and the cigarette they were smoking, which wasn't a regular kind. Crouching with his knees bent, a man at the center of the gang had his back to them. His hair was shorter than the others, barely down to the collar of his leather jacket, and he was working on his bike, scraping the tailpipe with a long, fat hunting knife. There was some burnt crud he was removing. Patrick looked closer and saw it was the melted-on remnants of a Wonder Bread bag.

"Hey, Mothman," the Viking called out to him.

*Mothman?* Patrick and Rex looked at each other. To hear those two syllables made Patrick's heart stop dead in his chest, then start again, hammering fast like an overworked minibike engine. They wanted to run. Patrick tried to jerk his arm free, but the Viking had them vice-grip tight.

"Wasn't that a Wonder Bread bag stuck to your tailpipe the day we all smelled like somebody pissed on us?"

Twenty-two-year-old Bobby Mauthmunn of Edgewoods, Illinois, stopped scraping. He didn't move. His knife blade leaned into the motorcycle tailpipe like it was a throat he was about to slice clean open. He was a Vietnam veteran approaching his goal of a hundred days. A hundred days without killing anybody new. It wasn't easy. He was messed up before the war, and the war had given him structure. Killing was the structure. The structure was good at first. But the structure had taken over. The jungle vines had grafted onto him, completely covering the person he had once been long ago, and now he was trying to pick them all off clean, one at a time, and not kill anyone ever again. This was his secret goal for the vacation, to reach Day 100 before the week was over. He was almost there. He didn't want any trouble. Patrick and Rex waited. They watched the knife. Without saying a word, Mothman rose up with his back to them. He stretched up about six-and-a-half feet tall, all lean and broad-shouldered, and blocked the sun. Then he turned around and looked at the boys with his tired, sad, *I-killed-a-lot-of-people* eyes.

"It was this one here," the Viking said, shoving Patrick toward Mothman.

Rex panicked. "It wasn't me. It was all him. Lemmie go!"

Mothman looked at the biker who still had a grip on Rex and nodded. He let Rex go.

Everyone looked at Patrick and gathered around. He could hear Rex's minibike start up and roar away. He was alone.

With his knife in one hand, Mothman took Patrick's chin gently in his other. He held Patrick's face like a pumpkin for carving, and tilted it up to see his eyes. They were boy's eyes. Patrick felt like a stranger was smashing into his bedroom, rooting through drawers, flipping over the mattress, reading his diary, knowing everything about him. Mothman knew Patrick was guilty, *so* guilty—guilty like the Viet Cong boy whose chin he had held in the same manner. That boy had helped the enemy with the ambush. It was a fact. Three members of his platoon had died. Three bloody bodies lay there beside the boy as Bobby Mauthmunn held his chin just so. And the boy might help others get killed when the platoon came back later. Killing that boy was a natural outcome, given the facts. It was structure. The boy had to die, like a squirrel caught chewing wires in the attic—a squirrel with boy's eyes.

"He told the whole thing," the Viking said. "We heard it, both of us." He nodded toward the woman with the long braid, the one who had quit her job holding the SLOW sign. She didn't like tourists anyway, so she snarled at Patrick. "It's true," she said. "He done it. Little shit."

Mothman looked at Patrick again. The A&W Root Beer stand had turned into a jungle hut. There were vines everywhere, flies buzzed over the bodies of his friends, and Patrick was the enemy. *Kill him,* the jungle whispered, its voice low and humid, tickling his ear.

"He pissed on us. Why don't we piss on him?" said the frizzy-haired woman who had ditched her waitressing job.

Some of them laughed. But Mothman said nothing. He just looked at Patrick some more and blinked. He let go of his chin.

The gang took that as a signal. They moved into action. A few of them pulled Patrick over near some bushes and shoved him on the ground. He tried to get up, but the woman who hated her waitressing job kicked him in the side and yelled, "Lay flat with your face down." She never got to talk to her customers like that. This was a vacation high point for her. Patrick lay still. This must be what it feels like, he thought, when you're old in a hospital bed, and the doctor walks in and says you're gonna die. Really? *Yes, I'm sorry, there's nothing we can do.* And then the nurse shuts the window so somebody outside walking a dog can't hear you scream. Get ready. No more arguing. No more prayers. It's over. He heard zippers unzipping. He pressed his face into the sand—a gritty, itchy sand—and started to cry. Hot urine was about to splash all over his hair and clothes. He held his breath.

What's taking so long? He heard a commotion.

"Shit," one of them said.

He looked around. The bikers were zipping up and boot-hopping off in different directions, because a witness—a girl with a dog—had just come flying down from the top of the sand dune. It was the girl from Indiana. She was chasing her little dog as it broke free and bolted down the dune in a joyous vacation escape, its leash flapping in the sand behind him. She was learning the hard way it's no good to let a dog lead you running down a sand dune.

"Sandy! Sandy!" she yelled.

Like sausage in a hot skillet, Patrick rolled over. He leaped to his feet. Right then—almost as loud as the girl from Indiana yelling, "Sandy! Sandy!"—a sound like swarming bees swelled up in his ears. It was Rex on his minibike with the engine whining. He came ripping around the back of the A&W. His face was leaning over the handlebars with a tight smile like it was grade school picture day. Later, he told Patrick, he had gone halfway up the hill and felt like shit, so he came back to see if Patrick was dead yet. With his engine red-hot, Rex skidded to a stop and almost hit Sandy. Patrick ran for the minibike and hopped on.

"GO!"

Off they went. Some of the gang were scampering for their bikes and cussing. Mothman stood still staring at Patrick, seeing a boy who didn't get killed. His fingers ached, remembering how they would have wrapped around his M-16, lifting it up to aim, pulling the trigger, feeling the kick as the bullet with a full metal jacket flew through the air, killing both boys with one shot through the back. It was Day 97. Three more to go.

# - chapter sixteen -

THE MINIBIKE TORE AWAY to the left while the girl from Indiana ran after her dog to the right. She didn't even know what had just happened. Certain the bikers were chasing them, Rex kept the engine open full throttle. The boys blazed up a narrow sidewalk for cottage renters strolling down to relax at the beach. Leaves, sticks, and branches whipped their faces. A grandmother in a 1930s bathing suit, humming a Fred Astaire tune, dove sideways into some honeysuckle, dropping her *Reader's Digest* as the boys shot past her. They stopped in the woods behind Rex's cottage by a big tree and listened. Nothing. No motorcycles. Rex cut the engine.

"WE MADE IT!" Patrick shouted.

"Shhhhhhh."

Rex whispered for Patrick to stay absolutely quiet and look around. Patrick looked from where they had just come. But Rex looked up in the trees, as if the attack might come from above. He went into a deep concentration about everything that had happened. No one was around and the woods were quiet and dark. Off in the distance Patrick could see the sun on some gravestones in the cemetery.

"Let's get out of here; we're OK now," Patrick said.

"Don't you know what just happened?"

"What?"

Rex told Patrick very solemnly that the biker nicknamed Mothman might be the *real* Mothman, and that meant, of course, he wouldn't give up. Rex explained that after Mothman had killed all those people in West Virginia, he might have joined a motorcycle gang to go about the country more freely killing other people. Patrick got into an argument over why, if he could fly, would Mothman go riding on a motorcycle, paying thirty-five cents a gallon for gas. Patrick knew the Mothman they met was only part of a gang that was probably back on the highway by now, leaving town. But Rex wouldn't listen; he knew more about these things than Patrick. Rex warned Patrick he should wear a disguise, maybe get a wig, and always wear sunglasses for the rest of the trip. And most of all, he warned, stay off of bridges. Patrick told him that's crazy.

"There's no such thing as Mothman, or UFO bases under Lake Michigan, or aliens kidnapping people for experiments," Patrick said. He spit to the side for emphasis.

"If there's no Mothman, then where do babies come from?"

Rex had him. If Patrick had missed the secret of the ages, then maybe he had missed some other things, too. But he told Rex not to talk about Mothman anymore the rest of the trip. Just forget it, or else he would ditch him, and Rex wouldn't get anywhere with Tammy, because she was always with Ginny, and Rex couldn't kiss two girls at once. Rex kept quiet but didn't promise anything. They agreed to stay off the minibike and meet up later at the Khardomah Lodge where Tammy and Ginny played the pinball machine. Patrick ran back to the cottage through backyards, keeping out of sight, and got there just a few minutes before the station wagon pulled in and Dad honked for Teddy and him to help bring in groceries.

"What have you boys been up to?" Dad said.

Patrick thought of his face in the sand and waiting for the biker gang to pee on his back. "Nothing," he said.

"Well, I'm glad you're learning how to sit still. Let's all help with the groceries, and I've got a surprise for your Mom."

"What is it?" Patrick asked.

"Shhhh, I'll tell you later. Now, go help your mother."

Patrick hurried over to the back of the station wagon and took a gallon of milk and a bag of groceries from Mom's arms.

"Why, Patrick, thank you," she said. She was more pregnant by the day and happy for the help. But when they got in the kitchen, she saw what was in the sink, and her mood changed. "Oh, no," she gasped.

The sink was a swamp of sooty beer cans soaking in water. While Patrick was gone, Teddy had been digging in the woods behind the cottage and found about ten old beer cans. To clean them off, he filled the sink with water and tossed them in.

"Patrick, what's this mess?" she said. "What have you done? This sink was spotless."

"Well, I—"

"Those are mine!" Teddy busted in. "I was digging for worms and found them. They're antiques for Dad."

Antiques? Dad heard one of his favorite words and reeled around.

"Why, look at this. These are old cone tops!" Dad said. "Teddy, did you and Patrick find these?"

"Yeah," Patrick said.

"*I* found them," Teddy said.

Patrick frowned his keep-the-secret look and noticed something terrible. Teddy was still chewing on the piece of gum Rex had given him. Teddy's molars were chewing on that gum like the ticking of a dynamite bomb about to explode. If Dad were to notice it after telling them NO MORE GUM for the whole trip, there would be a major court case with Teddy testifying how Patrick gave it to him to keep quiet about the minibike. As soon as Mom and Dad turned back to the sink, Patrick pointed at his teeth and mouthed the word "GUM!" Teddy caught on. He took the gum from his mouth and hurled it like a Bob Gibson pitch into the living room.

"You boys have got to get this mess out of my sink," Mom said.

"OK," Dad said. "I'll help. We'll put them out in the sun to dry." Dad winked at them, proud they were antiquing just like him.

They put away the groceries and had a little lunch. Patrick had a pickle loaf sandwich with some milk and half a banana. Mom cut up the other half into slices and laid them out on the high chair tray for baby Joey to eat. Next, she made a peanut butter and jelly sandwich with Wonder Bread and cut it into four slices to look like sailboats for Elizabeth. Dad cleared his throat and asked John to "show us your sculpture outside" and told Patrick and Teddy to grab a few of the antique beer cans and come have a look. Dad wanted them off to the side to talk about his secret. They went on the deck where John kept his modeling clay sculpture under a wet rag to keep it from drying.

"Show us how your sculpture looks," Dad said.

John unveiled it.

"What happened to Jesus?" Dad said.

"That was yesterday."

Today, the modeling clay was taking a new shape. It was a life-sized bust of John Lennon singing a Beatles song. John shaped the nostrils some more to get the right *Hard Day's Night* look while they watched.

"That's really good," Dad said. "You could be an artist some day and work for a big company downtown doing their advertising."

"I don't want to be a chump," John said. "I'm going to be a musician."

"Right," Dad nodded. Then he whispered, "Look, today's your mom's birthday and we want to surprise her with a cake and gifts. What have you got for her?"

The boys looked at each other and shrugged. Nobody had anything. Mom had let them down. There was nothing harder to remember than her birthday. It was the only birthday every year for which she failed to buy all the gifts.

"That's OK," Dad whispered. "We'll tell Mom we're going over to the driving range to hit some golf balls, but really we'll go into town to get her stuff for tonight."

"Can I go?" They all turned around. It was Elizabeth. She had sneaked up on them. Usually, Dad would say no when the boys were doing something secret. But after leaving her behind at the Burger Chef, he felt softhearted toward her.

"Well, all right, you can come with us, but you have to keep a secret. Can you keep a secret?"

"Yeah," she said.

"Well, I'll tell you what it's all about," Dad said. He went on whispering the secret, and Patrick noticed something about Elizabeth. She was chewing gum! He could see the red color of it. Teddy saw it, too, and his eyes bulged wide. It was the piece he had thrown into the other room. Dad was looking right at it, but he was so busy telling the birthday secret, he hadn't noticed it—yet.

# - chapter seventeen -

"GIVE ME YOUR GUM," Patrick warned Elizabeth as they walked out the cottage door.

"No, it's mine."

"I know, but you're not supposed to have it."

"It's mine. I found it."

"Shhhh."

He decided not to press it. They all got in the car to "go hit golf balls"—Dad, John, Patrick, Teddy, and Elizabeth—while Mom stayed behind with baby Joey. He was starting to pull himself up on the coffee table and walk around the edges holding on. Mom predicted that on this trip, baby Joey might even take his first real step out in the open. In the car, Patrick kept looking over at Elizabeth to see if she still had the gum, but she had already swallowed it. One piece wouldn't kill her.

"I can't believe it," Dad said. "Look, it's almost gone."

Driving along the ridge of the hill by the lookout, Dad pointed over to a balcony-wrapped lodge with concrete steps leading up to it. It was the old Hyland Park Hotel. Oddly, the steps were wider than the lodge.

"That's all that's left. I used to stay there when I was a boy with your Nana and Granddad."

"What happened?" John asked.

"They had a big fire a few years back. It used to be full of people all on vacation like us. Just think, most of those people I saw back then are dead," Dad said softly. Then Dad got quiet, because Nana was dead for a few years, and now Granddad was too old to make the trip. He was back home alone in Webster Groves, moving the sprinkler around a brown lawn and talking to the mailman.

"I'm sorry you can't have any good times anymore," Patrick said.

"These are good times, being with you all. We're all together."

They drove down South Harbor Drive past the State Park beach and the lighthouse and pier. Droves of people were out walking to the beach. And the road was peppered with motorcycle riders in black leather. Patrick kept low in his seat to avoid any trouble. Seeing the bikers reminded John that *Easy Rider* was playing this week.

"You have to let me go see that," John argued. "I'm old enough. I have lawn job money."

Dad laughed it off and said *no way*, because it was rated R.

"What's R?" Teddy asked.

"That means restricted," Dad said.

"But some of my friends have seen R movies," John said. He was in the front seat and really getting in some good points with Dad while Patrick, Teddy, and Elizabeth listened from the middle seat.

"In *this* family, children can only see G and PG movies," Dad said.

"But why?" John said.

"Because I said so."

Patrick knew the real reason. Movies were rated to hide the secret of the ages. Probably in that movie *Easy Rider*, they had a lot of motorcycle guys getting home runs.

"What's PG?" Teddy asked.

"PG? That's 'pretty gross,'" Dad said, laughing at his own joke. Dad always got in the best laughs at his jokes when he was trying to sidetrack everyone from an argument the kids were winning.

"Look," Teddy said, "a new movie is here."

They looked up Washington Avenue at the marquee hanging over the sidewalk in front of the Grand Theatre:

EASY RIDER (R) 9:30

HOOK, LINE AND SINKER (G) 7:00

"There's a G movie!" Teddy said. "Can we go?"

Dad studied the poster as they slowly drove by. It was a Jerry Lewis movie. "I don't know. Right now, we need to think about your Mom and getting her a present. She's a wonderful person."

As they strolled along Washington Avenue, the sidewalks were crowded with tourist families and a few bikers, some with chains attached to their wallets. The kids ran into Fortino's, a wooden-floored store with homemade candy inside slanted glass cases. Dad let everyone get one piece of chocolate for being good, and he picked out a box of chocolate-covered nuts for Mom. Smacking on caramels, they ducked into Steiner's Drug Store again—real fast—just so Dad could grab a birthday card, and then they crossed the street to go to the corner news stand, Hostetter's, where Dad wanted to get Mom a beach book.

Hostetter's News Agency, a two-story, corner building with fancy brick-work, was a proud outpost of civilization in the1890s. By 1969 the paint was peeling, and a Golden Retriever lay napping on the cool, blue-and-white checkered tile floor. Patrick petted him and breathed in the tempting smell of pipe tobacco and cigars. They had Prince Albert, Mixture 79, Edward G. Robinson blend, and more. Patrick felt ashamed that he had quit smoking with so much tobacco goodness all around him. The store was a paradise of nicotine, baseball cards, comic books, candy, Kodak film, and all the papers from big cities for vacationers to find out what they were missing—*The Atlanta Journal Constitution, New York Times, Detroit News,* and *Grand Rapids Press*. Wooden shelves were lined with magazines of every hobby including crossword puzzles, *Mad* magazine, hot rods, motorcycles, muscle building, fishing, and photography, all overlapping so that the cover girls kept one eye on customers walking by.

Over in the corner by the front counter, Patrick noticed a flash of nudity and spied a whole section of magazines with naked women on the cover. He had never seen anything like that back at Katz Drugs in St. Louis. He wanted to go right over there and find out more. But Dad was standing beside him, flipping through an *Antique Trader*. Dad was studying pictures of antique battle scenes, cigar posters, and tin Coca-Cola signs while in the corner a tourist man in plaid shorts and black socks was flipping through a naked women magazine mumbling to himself, "Uh-huh, uh-huh, uh-huh...."

"Wow, there's an auction of country store antiques in Manistee," Dad said, breathing heavily, "but we'll be back home by then."

The man in plaid shorts put down the naked women magazine without buying one and then bought a Milky Way bar. "I should eat a real lunch," he told the clerk, "but what the hell." He took a bite and walked out into the sunshine. The clerk standing behind a countertop display of Lifesavers closed the cash register drawer with a ding. Dad was not letting up on that *Antique Trader*, so Patrick reached for a paperback, any paperback, to kill some time. It was about Humphrey Bogart, the movie star. Patrick had recently seen him in *The Maltese Falcon* on TV. It was a detective story about a statue of a black bird that everyone wanted. In the movie, Bogart rolled his own cigarettes with no problem, even while he was talking on the phone. The paperback said he died of cancer.

Patrick shut the book and looked at the picture of Bogart on the cover. Bogart was dead. Wow. Patrick had always assumed Bogart was alive somewhere kissing a dame. He opened the book back up and looked at the pictures. There was one of Bogart at home by his Hollywood swimming pool, wearing fins and a snorkel. Bogart was bare-chested, grinning in the sun on a summer day, dripping wet, not yet knowing what destruction was coming. It made Patrick feel a little better that he had quit smoking. He had quit on Friday, the day before the trip, so Dad wouldn't catch him smoking on vacation. Back home, Patrick and his friends would all smoke on the tracks and discuss what to do next. He knew it was supposed to be bad for you because Dad lectured all the time against smoking, even though Dad had smoked for years when he was young and got away with it.

Dad bought an *Antique Trader* for himself and a James Bond book called *You Only Live Twice* for Mom. Patrick noticed the cover had a woman on her knees wearing a half open shirt with no bra. He could see the inner hillsides of her breasts.

"What's that about?" Patrick said.

"Oh, it's nothing, just a book moms like to read. You wouldn't like it." Dad asked the man to put the book in a brown paper bag and then changed the subject with Patrick. "We need to grab one more thing in town, and then get a cake over at Braak's Bakery."

They left Hostetter's and waited at the crosswalk for a funeral procession pulling out of the Dutch Reformed church. Somebody had died. Patrick wondered who he was, probably an old man from town who coughed his lungs out and got through the winter using liniments and balms from Steiner's Drugs but couldn't manage to make it through one more summer. When the crosswalk turned to "Walk," the funeral cars were still rolling by, so Dad grabbed Elizabeth's hand and told everyone to wait. Finally, it was clear.

"Say a prayer for the dead person's family," Dad said.

They crossed the street to the hardware store, and Dad rented a black-and -white TV for the cottage for a dollar a day. It was a lot of money, but he said Mom really wanted to watch her favorite show, which was on that night.

JEFFERSON COUNTY LIBRARY
NORTHWEST BRANCH

"Can we watch it?" Teddy asked.

"Oh, I don't know if you'd like it," Dad said, "It's a show just for moms."

Patrick knew why. Mom's favorite show was *Peyton Place,* which he remembered was about men in sports coats talking to beautiful women. He always got shooed out of the room by Mom, so he figured now the men and women in *Peyton Place* must have been working toward home runs.

To get the birthday cake at Braak's, they had to cross the Spring Lake drawbridge twice—once coming, and once going back. Remembering what Rex had told him about the Mothman, Patrick felt nervous both ways. Not really nervous, because he knew Mothman was made up. But what if he were real, just for the sake of argument?

What if the Mothman were lurking up in the girders, loosening bolts, and pushing on support beams? Ridiculous. Relax. Everyone else in the car was talking or listening to the song John was playing on the radio. "Time of the Season" was playing, which was a pretty good song if you weren't about to get killed. Patrick kept looking out the window for a winged man on the bridge, even though he knew there was no such thing. The car tires passed over the grated draw section, making a washboard sound. *This is it,* he thought, *we're going into the river.* He knew nothing would happen, and when nothing did, he felt stupid for even looking. He couldn't wait to tell Rex how there was nothing to worry about the Mothman. He'd tell him when he met up with Rex and the girls that afternoon at the Khardomah Lodge. That Rex, he didn't know everything.

# - chapter eighteen -

REX'S DOG CLYDE got skunked in the woods behind his cottage. It happened while Patrick was gone shopping for Mom's birthday stuff, so when he showed up at Rex's cottage to swing over to the Khardomah Lodge and meet the girls, Rex was sitting on the edge of the clawfoot bathtub in his underwear, with the dog standing in what looked like blood. Three big cans of Del Monte tomato juice lay empty on the bathroom floor and Rex was giving Clyde a tomato juice bath to get rid of the smell.

"What about the girls?" Patrick said.

"I'm almost finished."

The room smelled like skunk, even with the window open. Patrick figured they'd have to skip meeting Tammy and Ginny. But Rex laid out his plans while he and Clyde listened.

"You'll need a wig," he told Patrick.

"Are you crazy? I'm not wearing a wig."

"Shhhh." Rex whispered how they would both need disguises in case the Mothman and his gang came around to kill them. He told Patrick to look in the bathroom closet. And there was a woman's bathrobe on a hook, and on top of that a blonde wig.

"That's a girl's wig."

"You won't be the only one in disguise. I'll wear my Dad's golf hat and sunglasses."

"Why can't *I* wear the golf hat, and *you* wear the wig?"

It went back and forth like that, but Rex had a lawyer's answer for everything. He argued the Mothman knew Patrick on sight, but had only seen a feather glimpse of Rex. Patrick tried on the wig and looked in the mirror.

"No way. Whose wig is it anyway?"

"My mom's."

"Your Mom? What's she doing wearing a wig? She's got hair enough."

Rex laughed and trickled tomato juice down the dog's back. Clyde's tongue was hanging out, panting. He whispered it was something moms did when they got bored and wanted to look pretty at bedtime.

"I can't do it!" Patrick said, whipping the wig off and tossing it away from him as if it had cooties. "I'm not wearing your mom's home run wig."

"I'm trying to save your life. Trust me. We'll cut it with a scissors to make it shorter."

They walked up to the Khardomah Lodge in disguise. Patrick looked like the Dutch Boy paint can with his trimmed yellow wig, and Rex had on a straw golf hat and dark sunglasses. Patrick knew his disguise was no good. But then, as they were walking across the little wood bridge onto the gingerbread porch of the lodge, the screen door swung open, and out came the Confederate Army—Mr. Jawthorne, carrying a rifle. Patrick flinched and got ready to run, but Mr. Jawthorne nodded like the boys were strangers and turned to talk to the lady who owned the Khardomah, an older woman named Miss Gert.

"Have to shoot something this trip."

"Are you sure?" asked Miss Gert. "You're our guest."

"Just a few shots."

"OK, well, they're getting in somewhere up there," she said, pointing to the roof.

"I'll kill anything that moves."

Patrick and Rex moved to the side on the front porch. Very proud of their disguises, Rex jabbed Patrick and grinned. "It worked," he whispered.

Patrick watched Mr. Jawthorne with his rifle stalking into the woods along the side of the big, three-story wooden lodge. His feet were light on the leaves and his eyes up in the trees.

"What's he after?" Patrick asked Miss Gert.

"Squirrels. They're getting in the attic. You boys guests?"

"No, we're visiting some guests."

"That a real gun with bullets?" Patrick asked her.

She said it was just a pellet gun and held her hand over her forehead, shading the sun to try to spot any squirrels on the roof.

Patrick and Rex ambled past the screen door and into the dark-paneled lobby and saw Tammy and Ginny playing pinball by the Pepsi machine. It was a breezy, open window lodge with cushioned wicker chairs around the parlor, antique reading lamps with green-beaded shades, and guests in swimming trunks coming and going. In the hallway was a grandfather clock always ticking, pendulum swinging, with a smiling man on the moon face.

"Who's winning?" Rex said, disguising his voice deeper.

Tammy and Ginny knew who it was it right away.

"What are you doing dressed like a girl?" Tammy shot at Patrick.

Rex lied in his normal voice and told them it was a disguise so Mr. Jawthorne wouldn't recognize them. He left out the whole part about the Mothman. Rex was good at making decisions on what to say and what to leave out.

"Well, we've been waiting a half hour," Tammy said, cranking her hip out bossy.

Ginny was playing the pinball machine and not listening. The name of the game was Cinderella. The lighted glass scoreboard had artwork of Cinderella with blonde hair. She was pulling up her white dress, showing her legs, while a prince knelt at her bare feet holding a glass slipper for her to try on. There was a castle in the background up the hill where Cinderella would end up married. Patrick looked at Ginny.

Her arms were stretched out tight on the flipper buttons, and her long, blonde curls were jostling with each jolt of the flippers. "C'mon, get up there!" she said to the ball. Ginny was chewing bubble gum and concentrating. Her tongue was pushing out the pink of the gum to blow a bubble. But the game pressure got to her. She pushed too far and her tongue tip showed through the gum. Her ball went down the gutter.

"Dang-a-lang!" she said.

Patrick gave her another quarter and watched her play and thought about what it would be like to kiss her. POP. Outside, Mr. Jawthorne had fired the pellet rifle. The boys could hear him every few minutes let go another shot while they took turns playing pinball and talking about little stuff. Patrick was glad Rex was with him, because he didn't know what to talk about. Rex always had topics.

"I hope the aliens don't kill the astronauts on the way to the moon," Rex began.

"What?" the girls said, unaware of such things.

Rex lectured on how the astronauts were probably seeing UFOs for the first time and realizing they were powerless to protect themselves because the Apollo Eleven didn't have any machine guns, just some freeze-dried noodles and Tang.

"We have Tang back in Atlanta," Ginny said.

"The aliens aren't going to let us land on the moon without doing something to show they're more powerful," Rex said.

Tammy put her hand on Rex's shoulder—the first time she had ever touched him—and looked him in the eyes. "I get scared talking about that kind of stuff," she said softly.

Rex looked over at Patrick. Things were going well. Then without any warning, Ginny let go of the flippers, turned to Patrick and hugged him. His arms froze in her grip. She smelled of ChapStick and girl-scented lotions.

"Oh, prince, take me to the castle," she said in her southern accent.

Tammy laughed. Ginny's hug was just playacting, a Cinderella joke for Tammy. She let go of Patrick like it was nothing and then stretched and yawned. But to Patrick, this was a seismic event high on the Richter scale. His central nervous system sent instant replay after instant replay of the hug to his brain while he stood there trying to process it.

"We need to have some fun," Tammy said, stomping her foot. "Rex, have you got any money?"

"Sure, we got money. You want a soda?" Rex backslapped Patrick's shoulder and pointed to the Pepsi machine.

"We don't want no soda. We want you to take us *on a date*."

ON A DATE! Three words that when combined together could result in an explosion of kissing.

"A date?" Rex said like he'd found a five-dollar bill on the sidewalk.

Tammy put her arm around Ginny. "Look at us. The prettiest girls in Grand Haven and nobody to buy us a Pronto Pup or take us to a movie."

Just then they heard another pellet rifle shot outside.

"What about Mr. Jawthorne?" Patrick said, looking for the door.

"Don't think about him. Think about us," Ginny said, tilting her head to the side and fanning her lashes.

Then Tammy took Rex's hand and brought it to her lips, the way Cinderella might kiss a prince's hand. Rex turned his head so fast his hat fell off. But just as fast, Tammy pushed him away.

"YOUR HANDS SMELL LIKE SHIT!" she thundered. It was obvious she was Mr. Jawthorne's daughter when she got her blood up.

"I'm sorry," Rex said. "I had to give the dog a bath."

"Well, get cleaned up right, and meet us in town tonight at Pronto Pups."

"What time?" Rex said.

Right then Mr. Jawthorne opened the front door, carrying the rifle in one hand and two dead squirrels by the tail in the other.

"Six thirty," Tammy fired back, "and bring enough money."

Rex looked at Patrick. "OK," he said. "We'll be there."

Mr. Jawthorne saw the boys talking to the girls and stopped to let his eyes adjust to the dark. Rex picked up his hat, and they left in a hurry down the basement steps, through the shared kitchen, where a family from Ohio was boiling macaroni, then out the back way into the woods. To be safe from rifle shots, the boys ran off zigzag, and then drifted down to the beach so Rex could handle some dead fish and get rid of the skunk smell.

# - chapter nineteen -

"HAPPY BIRTHDAY TO YOU, Happy Birthday to you...."

The family celebrated Mom's fortieth birthday that Wednesday night. The candlelit cake flickered before her while Patrick, his brothers, sister, and Dad belted out the birthday tune at the dining room table in the cottage. It was six fifteen, and Patrick wanted to hurry up and get going into town to meet Rex and the girls.

"Forty years old," Mom said, tearing up, "I just don't know where the last ten years went, but at least I have all of you." She looked around at them, then patted the baby in her stomach and blew out the candles.

They clapped for her.

Then she blew her nose.

"Can I go now?" Patrick asked.

Dad frowned at Patrick and signaled for him to get the gifts. They gave Mom her card and candy and the James Bond book. She liked the book but didn't like the way Patrick was staring at the cleavage on the cover. So she put it up high. Then Dad threw in a pair of earrings he had brought from St. Louis, and when she thought it was all over, he disappeared to the car and came in with the black-and-white TV.

"I thought you might want to watch *Peyton Place*," he said.

"How very thoughtful of you!" Mom got up and hugged him. She dropped the open card on the table by the cake, and Patrick could see all their signatures on it, plus Dad had written his secret code: DYKW?

Once he had asked Mom what DYKW? means. She said it stood for "Do you know what?" That was what Dad asked her when they were dating, the first time he told her he loved her.

Somebody knocked on the cottage door. It was Rex coming to get Patrick. Dad let him in, and right away everyone smelled it. Rex had taken a shower and put on his dad's cologne to cancel out any leftover skunk particles.

"Rex! What's that you've got on?" Dad said. "Have you got a date?"

"Our dog Clyde got skunked, and I had to get rid of the smell," he said.

Patrick looked at Dad. That seemed to satisfy him. Rex was very clever at telling the truth in short bursts to offset a lie.

"Come on in and have some cake," Mom said. "It's my birthday."

Rex gave Patrick the *hurry-it-up* look and said, "No, thanks, we have to be going."

"Well, what's all the hurry? What are you boys planning on doing tonight?" Dad said.

"We're going to the lookout to count boats coming in and then maybe go over to my cottage to play checkers," Rex said.

"Why don't you boys play checkers here tonight, so we can keep an eye on you?" Dad said. He knew they were up to something.

Patrick and Rex looked at each other.

"Oh, no, not tonight," Mom said. "If I'm going to watch *Peyton Place*, we can't have boys listening in."

John plugged in the TV set and turned the channel knob to the *Peyton Place* station. The picture was snowy, but the *Peyton Place* theme music filled the living room, and Mom got excited. She moved her chair closer and handed baby Joey to Dad. He looked over at Patrick and Rex, as if he wished he could go with them.

"Whatever you do, stay out of trouble," Dad said.

They ran to the bushes where the Meijer's grocery bag was hidden with their disguises. Patrick put on the wig. Rex put on the golf hat and sunglasses. They laughed and jogged down the slanted sidewalk toward South Harbor Drive. With the two prettiest girls in Grand Haven waiting, they ran past the pier, the A&W Root Beer stand, and the Grand Haven Power and Light building. Along the way, they weaved around sunburned couples with moisturizer on their skin and clean-showered hair. Slow-moving cars and motorcycles hugged the Grand River leading into town. Up ahead, moths swirled around the light of the Pronto Pup stand where they saw Tammy and Ginny waiting. It was six forty-five.

"Where y'all been?" Tammy snapped. "You're late."

Rex blamed it on Patrick's family to smooth things over. "It was his mom's birthday," Rex said.

Ginny stretched her shoulders, cracking all her bones in line under her skin.

"Hi, Ginny," Patrick said.

Ginny said hi, but without much excitement. She was half thinking about a boy she had a crush on back in Atlanta and half wondering what smelled so pretty.

"What's that God-awful smell?" Tammy said.

"Oh, I put on some aftershave," Rex said.

"You never shaved in your life," Tammy said. She laughed in a mean way to entertain Ginny, who laughed along, too. "Now, who's gonna buy us a Pronto Pup?'

Rex looked at Patrick, and he got out his wallet. Between the two of them, they had about seven dollars and some change, plenty for a big night, but not much for the rest of the trip.

"This is my very first Pronto Pup," Ginny said to herself, holding up the hot dog on a stick dipped in corn meal breading and deep-fried. With the girls leading the way, the foursome walked over to Washington Avenue and hung a right for the Grand Theatre. The girls were nibbling and strolling while Rex slowed down a pace and whispered to Patrick, "Make sure we sit next to our dates, so we can kiss them during the movie when the time is right."

"How will we know when the time is right?"

"I don't know."

They got in line under the Grand Theatre marquee that hung over the sidewalk. The crowd was aglow in light from hundreds of round light bulbs. Posters under glass advertised the Jerry Lewis movie and *Easy Rider*, which came later. The girls stood in front of Patrick and Rex, talking to each other about other boys back home in Atlanta. Tammy wanted Patrick and Rex to be jealous, but they didn't care. Those other boys weren't here tonight. Tonight only Patrick and Rex would be sitting next to Tammy and Ginny to kiss them and feel their ChapStick lips. Patrick turned around to see how long the line was, and he couldn't believe it.

BOOM! The girl from Indiana was standing right behind him. Yellow hair, sunburned cheekbones, and blue eyes. MAN! She was not ten inches from his face. He stopped breathing. Her eyes were as blue as the bottom stripe of a Bomb Pop, the kind the ice cream truck sold back home when lightning bugs were blinking and kids would sprint across lawns shouting to moms for quarters. She was on a date with the two guys from the pier, but she looked into Patrick's eyes for a full second. The power of her eyes was something akin to what Betty and Barney Hill must have felt when they were abducted by the UFO on that lonely road and couldn't resist. He felt invited to spend the whole night under that theatre sign staring at her. But he forced himself to pretend he was looking over her head for somebody else and then turned back around to listen to Rex. He started breathing again.

"Let me tell you another secret," Rex continued.

Rex didn't know she was behind them, because he was busy talking about the Hollow Earth Theory. That was a theory that the top of the earth is never shown on TV news weather maps. "And do you know why?" Rex asked.

"No, why?" Patrick said.

"It's *be-cuzzzzz*, the government doesn't want you to know there's an opening up there, where all the UFOs come and go into the earth to their underground cities."

All Patrick could think about was the sad, caring eyes of the girl from Indiana. In their short, shared glance, he felt she knew him, even *understood* things about him he didn't understand yet, and she wondered if *he* understood *her*. He wanted to turn around and look again and hear more of what her eyes had to say. But then he remembered he had the wig on. Stupid wig. He looked like a fool. He wanted to take it off right there. Maybe she was only looking at him so tenderly because the wig made him look like a cancer patient with two steps between him and death.

"These things are all around us, but nobody but a few sees them," Rex said. He still had on his golf hat and sunglasses and looked like a fool, too.

Patrick pretended to listen, but he was secretly straining to hear what the two guys with the girl from Indiana were talking about. One of them was bragging about how his Mercury Cougar went a hundred miles an hour on the highway.

"Time to buy us our tickets," Tammy said, when she got up to the window.

Patrick and Rex pooled their cash for the ninety-nine-cent tickets and went in. The plush, burgundy carpet lobby led them toward the popcorn stand. Patrick kept walking. A tempting glass case filled with boxes of Goobers,

Raisinets, and Milk Duds grabbed Tammy's attention. She looked at Rex. Rex turned to Patrick to get at his wallet again, but Patrick had already moseyed on by to save money.

"Where do you want to sit?" Rex said when they got into the auditorium.

To get even for no candy, Tammy gave Patrick a huffy look and then filed into the row of seats first with Ginny beside her. When they all sat down, it was no good. Patrick was next to Rex, who was next to Patrick's date, Ginny, and Tammy was way over on the end next to Ginny. There was no way Patrick and Rex could kiss their dates. They were outfoxed.

The movie started. *Hook, Line and Sinker* was a comedy, but Patrick was too disgusted to laugh much. Jerry Lewis played a man who *thought* he was dying, but he really wasn't. He ran up a big credit card bill on a deep sea fishing trip, and then had to fake his own death and drop out of sight for several years because he learned he wasn't really dying after all. While Lewis' character was in hiding, his wife took up with his doctor friend, who had told him in the first place he was dying.

"Psssst," Rex whispered. "Look over there!"

Patrick looked. Five rows up a guy and girl were making out. He looked again. It was his brother John with a dark-haired girl. What? When did he meet her? Who's the girl? She looked different from the redhead he had been holding hands with on the pier. Patrick didn't know it, but the new girl lived in Grand Haven. She had come to the show to meet a girlfriend but ended up alone. That's when John had spotted her. Using his *Hard Day's Night* facial expressions and a large box of Milk Duds, John invited her to sit next to him. At first he only lightly kissed her on the cheek and she tried to fend him off, but then she turned her head toward him to kiss him on the lips over and over and over again.

"Look at them go," Rex whispered to Patrick.

"Yeah."

"He's only been up here a few days like us. What's his secret?"

"Something to do with the Beatles."

Suddenly, during a suspenseful spot in the Jerry Lewis movie, Ginny grabbed Rex's hand. Patrick saw it. What was she thinking? Ginny was Patrick's date. He elbowed Rex. Faking a cough, Rex let go of Ginny's hand to cover his mouth. He fake-coughed again to make it look convincing, then crossed his arms so Ginny couldn't grab him anymore.

The crowd roared, laughing. On the screen Jerry Lewis was flying down the street through traffic on a hospital gurney. Everyone in the theatre was having a good time, but not Patrick. It wasn't because Ginny was out of reach, or because John was necking and he wasn't. He was thinking about how the bikers had captured him earlier in the day, and how he only got away because of the girl from Indiana. He kept replaying the sight of her running down the sand dune chasing her dog, and then the sight of her blue eyes outside the theatre. Where was she now? He looked all around in front for her, but couldn't see her. He wished he could be with her, not to kiss her, but just to say thanks.

The movie ended with a giant swordfish stuck in Jerry Lewis' stomach on the operating table. When the lights came up, Patrick, Rex, and the girls all got up. Tammy and Ginny acted like they had a great time. Patrick and Rex smiled at them, then went into the men's room and tried to kill each other.

# - chapter twenty -

PATRICK TOOK OFF THE WIG and threw it at Rex and told him he owed Patrick about three bucks for all the money he'd spent on his stupid plan. Rex threw the wig right back at Patrick's face.

"Cheap ass! Why didn't you buy a box of Goobers or Raisinets?" Rex said.

"It's useless!" Patrick shouted, throwing the wig over Rex's head into the stall where they could see the tennis shoes of a guy sitting on the toilet.

"YOU go get that!" Rex growled.

"Get it *yourself!*"

Patrick turned to walk out, but Rex tackled him and they stumbled into the dome-shaped metal trashcan, the kind with a shiny flip lid. It fell over with a bang, spilling wet paper towels everywhere. The boys wrestled by the sink with red faces and hot eyes. Rex's dad's golf hat fell in the sink where somebody had left a quid with popcorn chunks in it. Rex reached to save the hat while Patrick quickly turned on the hot water, getting Rex's hand wet. With fast handwork and cussing, Rex put on the hat, which now had a distracting stalactite of sink spit hanging from the brim.

*"How do you like that?"* he said gritting his teeth and sloshing hot water in Patrick's face.

They death-gripped each other's ears, then for variety, Patrick mashed one hand in Rex's face, trying to push him back, while Rex barked out cuss words louder and louder.

"Hey, break it up. Dumb shits, what are you doing?" It was John rushing out of the stall. He had the wig in one hand and Patrick in the other as he separated the two fighters. Patrick was glad he was there, and he calmed down a breath.

John, who was that girl you were with?" Patrick asked.

"Yeah, great job," Rex said, catching his breath. "We saw you getting to first base."

"Shut up! Pick up that trashcan and be quiet!" he whispered. "You idiots are gonna get me caught."

Rex picked up the trashcan while Patrick kicked some of the paper towels behind it to hide the mess.

"Caught? Doing what?" Patrick asked.

"Yeah, what are *you* doing?" Rex said, looking around. They were alone, the three of them.

John looked in the mirror to straighten his Beatle hair style and told them, secretly, that he had only paid to see "that stupid Jerry Lewis movie" so he could hide in the stall and go watch some of *Easy Rider*, which was about to start next.

"What about your date? Is she gonna watch it with you, too?" Rex said.

"No, her parents won't let her. She had to go home. But *I'm* gonna see *Easy Rider*."

Patrick and Rex nodded. It was a good plan, and one whose craftsmanship they admired, but they still had dates out in the lobby and couldn't join him.

"What about Mom and Dad?" Patrick asked.

"They're watching TV and putting the little kids to bed," John said.

Just then, some bikers in blue jean and boots who had paid to see *Easy Rider* came in. They stood at the urinals, burping as they unzipped. They weren't the bikers they had dropped the Wonder Bread bag on. They were different. One of them said something about Vietnam, how a guy he once played little league with had just gotten killed over there. "Unreal, man!" Then the other one complained about maybe getting drafted, and they both cussed President Nixon while they peed. John eased back into the sit-down stall to hide until the movie started, but before he shut the door, he threw the wig to Rex.

"Let's not fight anymore," Rex whispered, tossing Patrick the wig as he walked out. "I don't want to hurt you."

"Maybe I'll hurt you!" Patrick called after him. He knew it was a weak comeback, but it was the best he could do. He stuffed the wig in his pocket and walked into the lobby.

Tammy and Ginny were waiting.

"What've you been *doing* in there so long, putting on *itchy bottom powder?*" Tammy said. "We're hungry."

"OK, how about Dairy Treat?" Rex said, knowing Patrick would pay for it.

Patrick didn't say anything. He trailed along behind Rex and the girls toward the front door. That's when he saw all the black leather and boots out on the sidewalk, bikers as thick as ants, buying tickets for *Easy Rider*. He whipped the wig out of his pocket and put it on crooked, as they walked out on the sidewalk.

"Are you having a good date so far?" Rex asked the girls.

"It's OK," Ginny said, cracking her neck.

Right there at the ticket window buying some tickets was the Viking and the braided woman who had caught them before at the A &W. Rex saw them and quickly put on his sunglasses, even though it was nighttime. They walked through the crowd, counting the seconds, expecting the long claws of the Mothman to land on their shoulders. Patrick had not seen Mothman, but knew he must be very, very near.

"There you are!" someone yelled.

They looked up.

It was Mr. Jawthorne. He burst from the crowd without warning like Jack Ruby gunning for Oswald. Out of nowhere, Mr. Jawthorne rushed them in the glare beneath the marquee. He was wearing white shoes, a blue-and-white striped summer suit, and a red bow tie. His face was red and his eyes were burning holes through Patrick and Rex as he grabbed them.

"*What choo mean* being out with these girls?" Mr. Jawthorne saw Patrick's wig was on crooked and knew it was a wig. He flicked it off, and then grabbed Rex's hat and sunglasses in the same swipe to get a better look at them. The whole crowd looked at them. The Viking biking couple turned around.

"Hey, it's them!" they said.

Before the boys could run, someone else appeared in the light under the theatre sign. Patrick's dad! He hadn't heard what was going on, so he approached the boys whistling the *Peyton Place* theme song in a pretty good mood.

"Patrick, am I glad to see you! Do you know where John and Teddy are?"

"John's inside … in the bathroom."

"Is Teddy with him?"

"No."

"Well, go get John, quick!"

Dad's order seemed like a handy one for the situation, so Patrick obeyed. It was his fastest display of obedience all summer. Dashing into the theatre, he left Mr. Jawthorne and the bikers and Rex and the girls out on the sidewalk.

"Now, what's this all about?" Dad asked Mr. Jawthorne.

"All about? I'll tell you what it's all about." Mr. Jawthorne went on a tirade to Dad about how these "Yankee boys" were trying to spoil his southern jewels, Tammy and Ginny. And the Viking jumped in, warning, "Boys who mess with bikers shouldn't be out after dark." Dad just listened, as if confronted with a surprise emergency at a Monday morning office meeting. He couldn't leave until John and Patrick came out of the theatre. The Viking poked his finger in Rex's chest, and then poked Tammy and Ginny, too, in case they were in on it.

That's when Mr. Jawthorne took the battlefield.

"WHITE TRASH!" Mr. Jawthorne yelled, swinging up a .38-caliber revolver from his pocket. The gun was an old companion from his over-the-road trucking days. Even now, as the owner of his own trucking company, he always kept the six-shooter in his glove compartment safe and sound under a Georgia map, in case he got a flat and had to fend off highwaymen in the night. Never once had he shot another human being, and secretly he braked for squirrels after Sunday worship service. But this was a moment of danger boiling to the level of the time in 1864 when two of Sherman's raiders stole kisses from two teenaged Jawthorne girls who had strayed into the woods fetching decorative pinecones. As the family story went, which Mr. Jawthorne had heard since his youth, the girls were unharmed only because of the bravery of fourteen-year-old Uriah Jawthorne, who mustered the last pony on the plantation to gallop after Sherman's men with a revolver and demand the girl's release. Now, Mr. Jawthorne found himself in almost the same plight, on vacation in Union territory, where his daughter and her friend's flowering womanhood was under attack. He was prepared to flash his pistol for the honor of the Jawthorne women. Showing his teeth, which were considerably raccoonish in their intensity, he waved the gun around at a wall of black leather and blue jeans.

Women screamed. The crowd peeled back.

"Ain't nobody gonna touch my Tammy and her friend!"

Patrick and John came running back out the front door of the theatre. Under the marquee lights, they saw the gun and went for Dad. He pushed them to keep running, with Rex and Dad running right behind them. They hopped in the Buick station wagon and drove off as Mr. Jawthorne herded Tammy and Ginny to safety and retreated to the confines of the Khardomah Lodge.

# - chapter twenty-one -

"WHAT THE HELL was that?" Dad said, speeding away. "We almost got killed!"

John, Patrick, and Rex all said they didn't know.

"Horseshit!"

Dad was mad, so they stayed quiet. He never used that word, except once after the Feast of Epiphany when the Master Charge bill arrived, totaling Christmas purchases. He was so excited and breathing so hard, the boogers in his upper nose were whistling.

"First thing we have to do is find Teddy. We'll talk about this later."

"Where is Teddy?" Patrick said.

"He's *missing*. Have you seen him?"

John, Patrick, and Rex all said no.

"Well, THINK where he might be. Think, boys. Think!"

They all looked at each other with wide eyes, shrugging. Patrick was relieved and happy they had a fresh crisis to deal with so they could have time to come up with a story of what had happened back at the theatre.

"Look out the window left and right as we drive. Your mother is worried sick."

They studied the crowds along Washington Avenue, but saw only tourists and bikers and people strolling with baby carriages toward the Musical Fountain. It was just now dark. The first squirts of colored water were fanning back and forth, and they could hear the faint sound of the funeral home man introducing the night's music.

"Good evening and welcome … tonight, a real treat, the music of *My Fair Lady*."

"Maybe he's at Dairy Treat," Patrick said.

"Dairy Treat? Good idea, I'll pull over and you go look fast."

Patrick got out and slammed the door, then turned around to ask Dad a question. "You want anything, maybe a small Butterscotch Joy or a dipped cone?"

"*Hell, no,* your brother's lost. Find Teddy."

"Right." He ran around Dairy Treat, scanning the crowd of teenagers in the orange moth lights for Teddy. He ran so fast he bumped into a teenaged guy, and they both fell over. The teenager fell into his hot fudge sundae, staining his Detroit Tigers sweat shirt.

"Stupid shit!" he said.

"Sorry," Patrick said getting up.

The teenager got up and tried to clean his sweat shirt with a napkin, but the hot fudge smeared into the fabric even worse. That's when he threw down his sundae in disgust, shoved Patrick, and cussed him out some more. Patrick looked again at him. He was one of the boys on a date with the girl from Indiana, the guy who had bragged about his Mercury Cougar going a hundred miles an hour. The girl from Indiana and the other boy came over from the walkup window. She pulled her spoon of soft ice cream from her mouth, failing to thoroughly clean all the ice cream from the surface. Usually, Patrick was grossed out when somebody left traces of spit-smoothed ice cream with lip streaks on a spoon. But she had so many other qualities, he didn't count it against her.

"GIVE ME A DOLLAR, SHIT FACE!" the teenaged guy yelled, shoving Patrick's shoulder.

"Don't be mean to him," the girl from Indiana said.

Patrick perked up.

"This asshole—"

"He's just a kid. Here, eat mine," she said, jamming her sundae in his chest. Some of her whipped cream got on the hot fudge already on his shirt. Her blonde hair rode the wind as she whipped her head about, and her blue eyes lit up mad enough to ignite her date's Mercury Cougar into a fireball that would be seen all the way to Muskegon. Patrick had to blink to stop from staring at her, she was so beautiful. She looked at Patrick, but didn't recognize him without his blonde wig.

"You better go, kid," she said.

"I'm sorry; it won't happen again," Patrick said.

Everyone was quiet. Patrick bowed thanks to her and ran off.

In the station wagon, Dad was livid that Patrick took so long and hadn't found Teddy. But then John got the idea that maybe Teddy went fishing.

"That's right," Patrick said, "he was digging for worms today."

"Worms? Good grief, he's probably been swept off the pier to Milwaukee. C'mon, let's go."

Patrick slammed the door, and Dad did a U-turn like Mannix with tires squealing and headed toward the pier. He only got a few blocks, though, when Rex spotted Teddy. He wasn't on the pier at all. He was fine.

"There he is, over by the Coast Guard docks!" John said.

They turned down a driveway into the Coast Guard area, off the Grand River. Teddy was fishing by himself under a streetlight. Everyone in the station wagon relaxed. Then something amazing happened that changed Dad's mood and made the boys forget they were in trouble. Teddy spotted Dad and waved like he hadn't done anything wrong.

"HURRY UP! IT'S A REALLY BIG ONE," he yelled. "HELP ME GET HIM IN!"

Dad, John, Patrick, and Rex ran from the station wagon down the grassy area to the spot where Teddy was wrangling his pole. The powerful Zebco rod arched and moaned in a struggle with a great fish.

"I said three Hail Mary's already, but I can't reel him in." He was all breathless and jumpy.

"Well, let me try." Dad grabbed the rod and said, "My golly, you've got a real fish here, Teddy. How did you catch him?"

"Everything you taught me, Dad! I said the Indian chant, '*Hick*-tah-minnicka-hannicka-sock-tah-*boom*-tah-*lay, Yoo hoo!'* And then I kept quiet and got a fish."

"That's terrific. You'll do all right. We'll get him in."

While Dad and Teddy were working the fish, John, Patrick, and Rex eased back a few steps to decide what to say later. The mosquitos were biting, and they slapped their arms and necks while they talked fast.

"Some parts we have to leave out," Rex said. Rex had a keen mind in a crisis, and John and Patrick were glad to have him along.

They settled on this: All three had just gone to the Jerry Lewis movie together and had only run into Tammy and Ginny there by coincidence. They decided to leave out the part about John necking like John Lennon with a town girl, and John hiding in the bathroom to see *Easy Rider*, and the part about the Wonder Bread bag and the bikers, and the part about the secret date with Tammy and Ginny and the contest to kiss them. Everything happened just as Dad saw it, but without the other stuff. That way, it wouldn't hurt Dad's feelings, and he could still trust them.

*"There he is!"* Dad hollered. "By golly! Look at the *size* of him!"

John, Patrick, and Rex ran over dockside and saw the fish roll near the top of the water and then go under. WOW. He was a white-bellied catfish, three feet long. They couldn't believe it. This was a monster, a wandering ghost, a King of the Grand River. And to think Teddy had hooked him solid all by himself with his new Zebco. He was caught. They flopped him into the back of the station wagon, gills moving, eyes wide open, with a row of hooks across the top of his mouth from other fishermen, lesser men whose lines he had snapped. Hurrying back to the cottage, they showed him to Mom who made everyone pose for a Kodak Instamatic shot by the kitchen sink. She was so proud, and Dad and all the boys were beaming with excitement. It was the high point of the trip, and nobody got into any trouble for what happened that night. Mom and Dad were in a forgiving mood. And then, Patrick's daydream ended. The line broke.

They all let go a death moan there by the dock.

"Damn," Dad said.

"He got away," Teddy said, his voice cracking a little.

They stood silent for a second and looked at each other. In the distance they heard violins from the Musical Fountain playing "I Could Have Danced All Night," while the arches of peach-lighted water reflected on the harbor dotted with pleasure boats. It was a sad and lonesome gut punch.

"I'll tell you what I'll do," Dad said. "Because you *almost* caught him, I'll buy everyone some ice cream at Dairy Treat."

The boys cheered. They jumped up and down. John, Patrick, and Rex carried Teddy on their shoulders up the hill to the station wagon. It was the biggest fish anyone in the family had ever almost caught, and it wasn't one of the big kids. It was Teddy all by himself. He was a man now.

# - chapter twenty-two -

WHEN THEY GOT BACK TO THE COTTAGE, smiling, laughing, and licking their spoons, Mom was relieved at first to see Teddy alive, but then she started a round of questions that led to the big argument: *Where were you , Patrick? Where were you, John? What? At the movie theatre? What? With two girls? And Teddy was fishing? At night? By himself? Without permission?* Patrick offered Mom the last few bites of his Butterscotch Joy to calm her, but she was too far-gone. "All liars will have their part in the lake of fire," she told Patrick. It was getting hot. Dad cleared his throat and said maybe Rex should go home to his own family, and Patrick knew then it was going to be the BIG ONE. Every vacation has one big argument, and this was it—Wednesday night, like a guillotine blade cutting the trip in half.

"This family is getting too far away from God," Mom began.

Patrick started to tiptoe up the steps to brush his teeth and go to bed, but she spotted him.

"YOU! PATRICK!"

"Yeah?"

"Get back down here."

He hurried back down. Mom told the boys and Dad to all sit where she could see them. They took up defensive positions in the wicker chairs in the knotty-pine living room, and Mom walked back and forth, very pregnant, making her case.

"We almost had one tragedy this trip with Elizabeth at Burger Chef, and now everyone is going their own way doing bad things."

"What bad things?" Teddy chirped.

*"Like sneaking out fishing!"* she snapped back. Her face was red, and her eyes were wide.

Teddy slunk down in his chair. Mom walked about, scratching her belly, outlining how Patrick and Rex had lied and said they were playing checkers, but somehow ended up in downtown Grand Haven with two girls.

"But—"

"And don't tell me you just *'ran into them there.'* I don't believe that for one minute."

She had him, and she was still building momentum. So Patrick kept quiet and waited for her to shift to John's sins. And that was the big one. She stomped into the kitchen and carried back something heavy covered with a wet towel.

"Look what I found in John's room!" She unveiled it.

"Mom, that's my art project," John gulped. "Be careful."

"Art? You call that art? It's not art; it's *nudity!*"

There it was. The lump of modeling clay that had started out as Jesus and changed over to John Lennon was now reshaped into a naked woman. It was better than anything Patrick had ever seen at the St. Louis Art Museum. She was a bosomy woman with hair down to her shoulders, posed sideways with her bottom showing and her legs tucked together, bent at the knees. Leaning on one arm, she held a real dandelion in her free hand while her big breasts hung swooping to the side. Patrick thought it was well done and couldn't wait to sign up for art class next school year. To get a better look, he leaned forward, but Mom saw him and snapped the cover back on.

"Did you do that?" Dad asked as if he were congratulating John for a game-winning buzzer shot at a basketball tournament.

"Yeah, it's just a nude."

"Why, it's as good as Michael Angelo," Dad said.

"Don't say that!" Mom said, losing steam and getting softer. "It's a naked *woo*-man. He's shaping a naked woman, right under our roof, while we go about cooking dinner and thinking everything's fine." Mom handed the sculpture to Dad and plunked down in a wicker chair to cover her face with her hand.

They sat quiet and felt bad for Mom. Dad lifted the towel to get another look and shook his head with a frown. He covered it back up and put down the sculpture on the coffee table and got out a downtown breath mint and started chewing so hard the boys could hear it cracking between his molars.

After about half a minute of the mint cracking and the waves landing off in the distance and the boys quiet, Mom looked at Dad.

"Aren't you going to tell them anything?"

Dad cleared his throat and talked softly. "All right, boys, I think you'd better get to bed now. Your Mom and I will decide what your punishment will be. We'll talk about this in the morning. Now, say goodnight to your mother."

John, Patrick, and Teddy filed past Mom sitting in her chair, the way they had filed past Lincoln's assassination chair at Greenfield Village. Her eyes were covered with her hand. John kissed her on the forehead and said happy birthday, and Patrick and Teddy did the same and went upstairs.

"That was a really good art project," Patrick said to John in the bathroom, brushing his teeth. "I like how you shaped her—"

"Shhhh," he said. "Listen."

They listened through the heat vent and could hear Mom and Dad talking downstairs. Mom said she had decided that all this goes to show that what the boys need is Jesuit high school. She told Dad they needed to get better morals and go to a high school without girls to shape their character and think more about God. Dad said he went to public high school and turned out all right. And besides, he said, with what they charge for tuition, those "Jevies have a racket going."

"Don't you care about their souls?" Mom said.

"Of course, you know that."

"Well, what about this sculpture?"

The boys listened a long stretch for Dad's answer. Maybe he was lifting the towel again to study it more. Then they heard him speak up. "I'll tell John to sculpt some clothes on her in the morning. She'll be all right with clothes on, won't she?"

"You need to talk to John and Patrick about girls."

The boys got in bed and heard some more through the floorboards of the old cottage. Mom said her decision was final. Out on the pier, the fog house horn sounded a long, worried note for ships lost in the lake. Mom was going to pray for some way for the boys to go to a Jesuit high school to save them from the world and from themselves. Dad said maybe Mom should get a job herself, if she thinks money is that easy to come by. He told her to not be too sure about the future.

"What if I were to drop dead? How would you pay for all of this?"

They argued some more, but Patrick fell asleep before it was over. He didn't know what punishment the morning would bring.

# - chapter twenty-three -

THEIR PUNISHMENT WAS SEVERE. Dad decided he would take the boys antiquing. They looked at each other and out at the lake. The water was raging and alive. It was a red flag day with high winds and giant waves, perfect for body surfing and getting thrashed around. *Do we have to go today?* they all asked, pleading to go to the beach. Each one tried to talk Dad out of it, but Mom's arms were folded shut. She said they needed to do some penance and mature. Besides, she said, red flag days are "too dangerous" because the waves come crashing in at an angle and keep pulling the older kids down the shore away from where she's babysitting Joey and Elizabeth. Being so pregnant, she didn't want to have to lurch up and waddle down shore yelling, "GET BACK HERE WHERE IT'S SAFE!"

"We'll be back around dinner time," Dad said grabbing his *Antique Trader* and Michigan map.

"Do you know where you're going?"

"I'm not sure yet. But I'll try to be good." He kissed her goodbye, the short kiss of a collector to a non-collector, and got in the car.

"Don't waste any money," she called out, "and be careful, and don't be late for dinner … and be sure to talk with them about *what we talked about*."

They hated to hear that last part. John, Patrick, and Teddy filed into the station wagon and fell silent. Their punishment would be a lecture *and* antiquing. Patrick had been antiquing plenty of times with his dad. Dad loved escaping down country roads to barns full of old stuff. Some white-haired couple would lean back in chairs while Dad looked at their spider-egged furniture, or rusty beer signs, or Civil War battle scenes which Dad inevitably thought were "really terrific." Usually a farm cat would tiptoe across the white gravel barn floor prowling for mice. Then the old people would moan about their knees or how cold a winter it had been while Dad would haggle with them to lower their price for some junk that ended up back home in Dad's basement. Dad used antiquing to relax from his job downtown where he had to wear a suit and tie, and his boss would grit his teeth and yelled when sales charts pointed to the floor. Pulling away from the cottage, Dad was in a bright mood.

"Boys, to the open road!" he smiled.

Patrick looked over at Rex's red cottage as they drove away. Here it was Thursday, and he still hadn't kissed Ginny. Wasting a day antiquing would mean, he would only have Thursday night and Friday.

John turned on the radio to the song, "In the Year 2525." The station wagon passed a blueberry field where an automatic sprinkler shot a soft arc of water on the blueberries like a clock—*tip, tip, tip, tip, tip, tip*. There was a bright red barn and a farmer in the yard with two kids.

"Look at that," Dad said. "The paint on the barn shows the state of the farm."

"What?"

"If the barn is in good shape, it means the father is still alive." Despite themselves, the boys all turned to look.

Turning inland, Dad took them farther away from the lake and vacation happiness, down a two-lane road with no people for miles, just woods on either side. The wind through the open windows ruffled the pages of the *Antique Trader* on the car seat, and the song on the radio made everyone quiet, thinking about the words. In the year 2525, nobody can say who will still be alive. Patrick didn't say it out loud, but he added up the math and figured that everyone in the car would all have been dead for about five hundred years. It gave him a shudder, so he put it away for now.

"Look over there," Dad said.

They looked and saw another barn with no paint left, the gray wood warped from the rain. Wild brush tangled up through one side that was missing some boards, and there was no crop in the field.

"It's a sad reminder," Dad said.

"What are you talking about?" John said.

"Somebody must've died. You just hope the family survived somehow. Boys, I want to talk with you about women. Now, your mother and I—"

"What's that up ahead?" John interrupted.

They all looked.

It was a prison. Dad slowed down and drove past a fortress-like building with barred windows, and behind each window was a man dreadful sorry he'd shot somebody or robbed a liquor store. Patrick felt sure somebody inside the prison was watching the station wagon, maybe noticing his arm resting by the open window, jealous that Patrick could drive by feeling the breeze while the prisoner was locked up.

"Captivity! It's a curse," Dad said. "I wonder what's happening back at the office." Dad was quiet, remembering a big project waiting for him on his desk. He got out a downtown breath mint and crunched on it.

"Now about women…."

But before he could get going, the trees parted on a town with a row of antique shops. It was one of those red brick main streets with cars parked at an angle, and fancy storefront buildings with 1896 or some ancient year chiseled in the top stone. They got out and walked down the sidewalk past some plaid shirted, corncob pipe men sunning themselves on a bench. Dad said hello, and they nodded very friendly and watched the boys bring up the rear.

"Don't break anything," Dad said as they entered the antique shop.

A naked picture of Marilyn Monroe on a tin tray was on display behind the counter. She was a movie star lying on a red blanket with blonde hair and very big breasts. John and Patrick saw her right away and looked at each other. Teddy didn't notice. He was shorter and looking into a display case of antique fishing lures down at his level. John and Patrick looked at Dad. He was talking to a white-haired woman behind the counter with the Marilyn Monroe tray right above her head.

"Yes, Ma'am, I wonder if you could help me. I'm looking for old Civil War battle scenes," Dad said, getting out another downtown breath mint.

"Prints?"

"You know, big colorful scenes you can enjoy from across the room."

John and Patrick stood staring at the Marilyn Monroe from across the room.

"We had some," she said, scanning her shop cluttered with oak washstands, a spinning wheel, kerosene lamps, and a deer head with antlers on the wall.

Dad turned to study where she looked, but John and Patrick stood like sentries guarding that Marilyn Monroe tray.

"Good stuff goes fast. A man up Grand Rapids way collects them. He came through here."

"Brother." Dad looked at John and Patrick, and for the first time he saw what they saw. Like a rifle shot, he snapped his fingers to get their attention, and then motioned for them to look around the shop at other things. Turning back to the woman, he asked, "I wonder if I could trouble you for his name?"

"Well, we can't give out customers' names."

"It's all right. This is just a hobby. These are my boys. I'm trying to get them interested in history."

She looked at Teddy and said OK.

Dad was good at talking to strangers at antique shops and using his downtown executive skills to get information on where to find junk. They drove over to Grand Rapids, looking for the house of the man with Civil War prints, while Dad brought up the subject of naked women again.

"Look, boys," he said working up a way to talk to John and Patrick without educating Teddy, "I need to talk to you about girls, now that you're getting older. What grade are you in?"

"I'll be in sixth grade," John said.

"I'll be in fifth grade," Patrick said.

"I'll be in third," Teddy said, "but Dad?"

"Yes, Teddy?"

"I have to go to the bathroom."

Dad told him to hold it until they got to the man's house, but they couldn't find the street and pulled into a Sinclair station with a green dinosaur, and Teddy got out to go pee. They watched Teddy go into the men's room and close the door.

"I wonder where this street is," Dad said, unfolding the map. John and Patrick tried to help him, because now that he was in his forties, Dad's eyes were getting long-armed. But the boys couldn't find it either. So Dad told Patrick to call out his window and ask directions from a man looking at the tires on his pickup truck.

"I can't do that," Patrick said. "He's a stranger."

"Don't be afraid of life," Dad said, tooting his horn, and waving for the man to come over. The man started walking toward them. Just then they saw

Teddy coming out of the bathroom. He ran straight for the Sinclair dinosaur and tried to climb on it. Dad turned to John and Patrick. "Look, boys, real quick before Teddy comes back, you shouldn't think about naked women until you're married and maybe see your wife on your wedding night."

John and Patrick looked at each other and then back at Dad.

"And even now, don't look at a girl and see just her body. You should see a girl *as a person*. You understand?"

"As a person?" Patrick said.

"That's right; a girl is a person."

They nodded and pretended to understand. And before Dad could say another word, Teddy got in the car and then the man Dad had honked for came up to Patrick's window.

There was a hole in the man's throat.

Death, disease, and horror leaned in the station wagon, inches from Patrick's eyes. The hole was just above his plaid shirt collar, the size of a bathroom sink drain. Around the edges was a ring of bumpy scars from where the surgeon had cut him. He spoke in a raspy, voiceless way like a monster at a gas station.

"We're looking for a street," Dad told him. Patrick couldn't hear what the man was whispering over the roaring sight of that hole. To see it up close was to peer over the edge of a freshly dug grave, dark and deep and ready to be filled. Dad understood him and thanked him and they drove off. The boys were quiet for quite a few blocks, and then Dad said, "Boys, that's why you never want to smoke."

# - chapter twenty-four -

SMOKING A BOWL of vanilla pipe tobacco, Gordon Finley greeted them at the screen door of his Grand Rapids bungalow with a smile and a parakeet on his shoulder. He was a short, thin man with shoulder-length gray hair, a goatee, baggy pants, old shoes, and a button-up sweater with pockets that overflowed with crumpled napkins and brown pipe cleaners. Dad introduced himself and explained about the Civil War prints.

"I'm a collector like you, and these are my boys."

"My God, you brought an army. Come in."

"Thank you." Dad motioned the boys to follow him. They entered the living room where the parakeet took flight and circled around before landing on a curtain rod to study the visitors. A woman with wooden crutches at her side sat in a saggy reading chair, fanning herself with a folded-up newspaper. The black-and-white TV was on. A *Perry Mason* rerun was just starting, and the opening theme song raced to an ominous cliff as she turned to look at the boys. *Bah-nahhhhhhhhhhhh-DAH-DUM! Bah-nahhhhhhhhhhhh-DAH-DUM-DUM!*

"This is my wife, Mrs. Finley."

"How do you do?" Dad said. He nodded to the boys, and they lined up to shake her hand. Mr. Finley eased over to the TV and switched off *Perry Mason*. It was quiet.

"Three sons!" she said, smiling with crowded teeth. "And they're all so *alive*. You want some water?"

They said yes, and she turned to Mr. Finley.

"Gordon, can you please?" Her feet were diseased, so Mr. Finley scrambled into the kitchen.

While he was gone, she talked over the chirping parakeet about the summer heat, fanning herself with the *Grand Rapids Free Press*, which Patrick noticed was folded open to the obituary page with columns of dead people. "Gordon hasn't turned on the air conditioner once this summer," she whispered. "You know, he had to retire early when the printing company shut down." She went on about how the neighborhood was changing. A maple tree forty years old died, and the woman next door was now a widow. "She's in a band and stays out until all hours with different men." Dad fidgeted and looked around.

Above the mantle was a framed poster of the silent movie cowboy, Tom Mix, looking at them with guns drawn. All the lamps were off. Tired sunlight came in the open windows, but no breeze. They could hear a lawnmower coughing down the street, and the room smelled like old pipe tobacco mixed with attic heat and musty furniture. Patrick thought of how breezy and carefree the lake must feel right now with Rex and the girls body surfing. Foaming, curling waves tossing Tammy and Ginny into the sandy shallows and Rex laughing and smiling, helping them up, holding their wet, suntanned arms.

"Drinks on the house," Mr. Finley said, returning with four mason jars of ice water. He gave them each one and then whooshed into his reading chair, which had coffee slop marks on the armrests and scuffed up wooden hoof legs. He put more tobacco in his pipe and flicked a Zippo lighter that made locomotive flames and smoke rise up toward a brown stain on the ceiling above his chair. When it was going well enough, he tucked the tobacco pouch neatly between his armrest and the seat cushion. The parakeet started chirping and flew back on Mr. Finley's shoulder.

"So, you collect?" Mr. Finley said. He was in a good mood, happy to have visitors.

"A little bit … old prints, battle scenes."

"Finding anything?"

"Not much, but it's fun just looking."

"Ah, the thrill of the hunt. You're right there. It's not the having, it's the getting."

"Yes, it's just very relaxing to take my mind off work and enjoy life."

"I agree. Collecting is one of the joys of life."

"The man down the street died over the winter, and they sold all his possessions at an estate sale," Mrs. Finley said. "Even his shoes. Now his house is for sale."

They all looked at her, and at their shoes, and sipped their water.

"Well, it sure is nice of you to have us in. I hope we're not interrupting anything," Dad said.

Mr. Finley took the pipe out of his mouth to say something friendly.

But Mrs. Finley cut in. "Oh, you're not interrupting anything. Gordon was just smoking his pipe, and I was reading the paper."

"You mean reading the death notices," he chuckled.

"Gosh, I hope we didn't come at a time of tragedy," Dad said.

"No, we haven't got any tragedy, except the electric bill." Mr. Finley laughed a little at his joke with a Michigan kind of easiness. "She pours over those damned funeral notices every day, hunting for other people's tragedy. It takes the birdsong out of life."

Mrs. Finley took a deep breath to prepare for battle. The parakeet took off again, leaving the room the way animals flee before an earthquake.

Mrs. Finley gripped her obituary page and leaned forward like TV lawyer Perry Mason about to pound out a murder case. "There's more to life than birdsong and collecting!"

"Here we go," he said, picking lint off his sweater and then looking at the boys in the jury box on the sofa. "Marriage can be a beautiful thing, boys. It isn't always like this. When you're young and can go dancing, why then—"

"But we're *not* young! And we *can't* go dancing!"

They all looked at her crutches.

"The man across the street died. The maple tree died. Where will we be in ten years?"

"I don't know," Mr. Finley sighed. He was really puffing that pipe now, and the smoke was hazing up around the picture of Tom Mix with guns pointing down on them.

"Tell me, if you can, what's ahead?" she said, cross-examining him.

"We fight like cats and dogs. It's old age," he said to Dad.

Dad nodded.

Mrs. Finley wrapped the obituary section on her knee. "It's right here. Look!"

They all looked at her tapping her finger on some dead guy's name.

"Dead people would probably tell you, if they could, that death is much bigger than we know. When you're dead, you're dead for ten million years.

And that's just the first page of a story that's thicker than the phone book." She reached by the end table, grabbed the Grand Rapids phone book, and lobbed it on the rug to show her point. It landed in the middle of the living room with a thud and curled half open. Then she rooted around a drawer next to her in the end table.

"Oh, please, dear, not the tape measure," Mr. Finley said.

They all looked over at her. "Here, pull out the end of this," she said, holding a shiny tape measure toward Patrick.

He got up and pulled out the metal tape measure a few feet.

"Back farther. We need seventy-four inches."

"Why seventy-four inches?" Dad asked.

Patrick walked backwards until she told him to stop.

"The average human life span is just seventy-four years," she said. "Think of that in inches. "Now, you boys are way down the line in what looks like the safe zone at maybe ten inches or so, but it goes fast. Gordon and I are way up here in our late sixties. Look at how few inches we have left."

Mr. Finley closed his eyes and squinted hard.

"We're almost to the end of the line, and you know what happens next?"

"No, what?" Patrick said.

"Let go," she said.

She pressed a button and the tape measure SHOT from Patrick's fingertips back into the holder. "After that, you move to the phone book." She looked down on the floor at the phone book and sighed. "You boys want some more ice water?"

"Oh, hell, you don't want to hear all this," Mr. Finley said, leaping to his feet. "Let's go look in the basement and enjoy life."

They followed the blaze of his pipe toward the dark kitchen, and Mrs. Finley watched the boys—their shoes, and hair, and faces—measuring their youth and life span. She probably would have come after them to say more, except for her diseased feet and the crutches. They walked past a little breakfast table with two plates and some sad, uneaten bread crust.

"Watch your head," Mr. Finley said, going down the steps.

They followed him in the dark, down wooden steps with rubber tread guards into the cool of the basement. Then Mr. Finley reached up and pulled a string, and on came the light.

It was an old light bulb from 1918—the kind Patrick had seen in Thomas Edison's workshop at Greenfield Village. Mr. Finley said it was fifty years old and still working, but he said he always worried one day he would pull the string and it would flash out.

"By golly, where did you find all this stuff?" Dad said, looking around. He was really excited.

"Oh, here and there, along life's highway."

Mr. Finley cranked up a Victrola record player. Ragtime music filled the room. One side of the basement looked like an 1890s general store complete with a wooden counter, a red coffee grinder, and a brass cash register, and behind that, shelves from floor to ceiling lined with coffee tins, medicine bottles, a wooden cage mouse trap, and antique toys. There was even a tin sign showing Abraham Lincoln advertising a five-cent cigar. Dad was the happiest he had been the whole trip.

"Gordon, this is *terrific*!" Dad said.

"And all collected on a printer's salary," he said.

Mr. Finley relit his pipe and strolled about showing them another side of the basement with five-cent machines from the Romona Amusement park for viewing primitive movies captured on hand-cranked flip cards. One showed a chorus girl dancing, another Charlie Chaplin walking with his cane. There was also a small room with a six-seat theatre with rows of wooden movie house seats and red velvet curtains draped around the screen. Hanging on the wall was a giant poster of a man dangling from the hands of a clock high on the side of a skyscraper while a woman on top of the building reached out to try to save him.

*Safety Last* was the name of the movie. Patrick and his brothers had never heard of it.

"That was Harold Lloyd. He was a big star," Mr. Finley said.

The boys got bored after a little while, and Mr. Finley told them to go scout around the backyard to see the goldfish pond. "Just don't scare the fish," he said.

"And don't drown," Dad added. John, Patrick, and Teddy ran upstairs and out the back door.

It was hot outside. Teddy went right for the fish, trying to catch them with his hands, while John and Patrick rooted around the garage, putting on hats and looking at an old Desoto with a flat tire. There was also a black-and-white poster of Lauren Bacall on the garage wall. "If you need anything, just whistle," the caption said. She was Humphrey Bogart's girlfriend in some of the movies Patrick had seen. Later they got married and had two children, but then Bogart died. The boys climbed in the Desoto, all three of them, pretending they were bank robbers, with Teddy behind the wheel. Teddy got so excited about being able to drive that he let out a silent fart, which soon expanded and sent John and Patrick tumbling out the side doors to safety. They were all three laughing, having a good time, but Patrick wished he could hurry things up and get back to the beach to catch up with Rex and the girls. So he went back inside by himself to prod Dad along.

Halfway down the steps he stopped and listened. Dad was saying something to Mr. Finley. They were in the movie theatre part of the basement by the *Safety Last* poster. Patrick could see their legs, but they couldn't see him.

"You should quit now, before it gets you," Dad said.

"Oh, I've smoked so long, I can't quit. I'm like a fiend."

"I smoked for eighteen years, but as soon as the Surgeon General came out with the news, I quit."

"That's good."

"But it may be too late for me."

"What do you mean?"

That's when Dad told him. He whispered the secret. Before the trip, he was having sore throats so bad he went to the doctor for tests. Patrick wanted to cover his ears or run outside. But he couldn't move. He sat there halfway down the steps with his hands wrapped around his legs and his chin between his knees.

"What'd they find, cancer?" Mr. Finley said.

"I don't know."

"You don't know?"

"Not yet; I told them not to tell me."

"Why not?"

"If I have to die, I don't want to know until after the vacation."

"Do your boys know?"

"No, don't say anything. Not even my wife knows. Just me and the doctor."

Hot tears came to Patrick's eyes, and a dizzy feeling like right before vomiting. How could this be happening to him? He was only eleven. Dad was going to die? He shot up and tiptoed back up the steps and opened the back door and ran straight for the pond. John and Teddy were in the garage, so they didn't see him crying. He fell down on his knees in the grass and plunged his head under water, yelling, "NOOOOOOO!" Angry, pleading bubbles poured out his mouth, and he could hear himself shouting under the water at God. Fish dove deep into the pond grass and mud. After he came up wet-faced, Patrick saw John and Teddy standing there laughing. They couldn't tell he was crying. They thought he was fooling around, or just hot, because his wet face hid the tears. He dried off his face with his shirt. Then Teddy stuck his head under water, and John tried it, too. They all three did it together, screaming under water. But only Patrick knew the secret. John and Teddy came up laughing, and Patrick came up fake-laughing with them, their faces dripping in the sun.

# - chapter twenty-five -

MOM'S FACE WAS COVERED WITH MUD when Patrick walked in the cottage. It had been a long ride back with John sitting in front seat with Dad while Patrick was stuck in the middle seat with Teddy. Patrick wished John was next to him, so he could tell him the awful secret. He couldn't stand it. But as the ride wore on, Patrick decided he shouldn't tell anyone, not even John. Why ruin John's vacation, too? Why make Teddy cry? Why make Mom cry when she found out? Why turn the rest of the vacation into the wake that he was feeling? Dad asked Patrick in the rearview mirror why he was so quiet. He looked out the window at a collapsed barn and felt the pinprick of tears biting his eyes and nose. Then Dad made a joke about how Patrick was probably sad he missed having a date with some girl at the beach. Everybody laughed and Patrick fake-laughed with them.

Walking into the cottage first, Patrick saw Mom sitting in the living room in her favorite wicker chair. There was a woman leaning over her smearing Mom's face with mud from a jar. He looked again. It was Mrs. Jawthorne. Then whipping his head to the left, he saw Mr. Jawthorne sitting in a side chair all comfortable, nibbling one of his unlit cigars. He eyed Patrick. Patrick looked back at Mom.

"I'm getting a treatment," she said. "The Jawthornes came over for a visit, and Mrs. Jawthorne brought me a jar of … what do you call it?"

"Atlanta Mud Balm. It's restorative. Keeps a woman young forever." She was swirling it around Mom's cheeks and eyes.

"Jar says it'll take away crow's feet," Mom said.

Patrick nodded and looked over at Mr. Jawthorne. The other night outside the theatre he was charging with bayonet mounted. Now he was at ease, but his eyes flickered with a readiness for battle. Patrick wondered what would happen when Dad came in to meet him. Dad, John, and Teddy were still out at the car getting things to bring in. Baby Joey had pulled himself up to stand alongside the coffee table, and Elizabeth was at Mom's feet, holding Betsy Wetsy and watching the mud treatment.

"About the other night," Mr. Jawthorne began.

"We came over to apologize for the shameful way Mr. Jawthorne waved around his pistol when you and that other boy … what's his name?"

"Rex."

"When you and Rex was just showing good manners and company to our Tammy and her friend Ginny," Mrs. Jawthorne said. "Isn't that right, dear?"

Mr. Jawthorne shifted in his chair and bit off another nub of the cigar. "I guess I might've galloped a step too far, *suspecting things*."

"That's right," Mrs. Jawthorne said, massaging Mom's muddy face with more muscle. "It's not like they was out trying to *kiss* our girls. They was perfect gentlemen."

"I guess you're right. I … I apologize," he said with his head down. "Maybe I was wrong about you and your attitude toward us being from Atlanta." He stood up and reached out to shake Patrick's hand.

Patrick took a step toward him when Teddy stumbled through the door carrying a big tin sign Dad had bought from Mr. Finley's basement. It was a five-cent cigar sign showing the face of President Lincoln with a slogan at the bottom that said, "With malice toward none and charity for all."

Mr. Jawthorne drew back his hand and mumbled, "Lincoln!"

"Oh, that's nothing. Just some junk my husband bought," Mom said. He likes antiques and goes—

Right then, John walked in carrying a big framed lithograph of Sherman's March to the Sea, showing General Sherman on his horse pointing toward Atlanta with his troops twisting railroad ties and burning barns along the way.

"And the devil Sherman!" Jawthorne growled.

"Oh, that's just his hobby," Mom said. "I don't care for history, do you?"

Then Dad walked in carrying a framed poster of General Lee surrendering his sword to General Grant at the Appomattox Court House, with all Grant's staff looking on.

"INFAMY! I won't stand for this! Let's go!" Mr. Jawthorne thumped his wet, tooth-marked cigar on the rug and walked out, turning to his wife and shouting, "Come along now, Clarissa!"

Mrs. Jawthorne shrugged and told Mom she had a wonderful visit and hoped she liked the mud balm. Then they hugged ,and Mrs. Jawthorne winked at Patrick, nodded to Dad, and scurried out the door.

They all looked at Mom. Her face was all muddy and her mouth was open.

"What's going on here?" Dad said.

"They came over to apologize, and something went wrong."

"I don't think he likes antiques," Teddy said.

"Look!" John said pointing at baby Joey.

Letting go of the coffee table, baby Joey turned toward Dad and took his first step.

The astronauts had not yet stepped on the moon. But they were getting closer. It was Thursday night, and Rex promised Patrick they were closer than ever to kissing Tammy and Ginny. But after what Patrick had overheard that afternoon—the awful secret about his dad—he wasn't in the mood to kiss anybody. Everything and everybody seemed like a TV show he was looking at but not watching. Rex thought he was just scared to kiss Ginny. To bring Patrick out of it, Rex rubbed his shoulders like a coach before a boxing match while they sat in Rex's bedroom rehearsing the plan. The door was shut, and Rex had laid out on his dresser the things they needed to create the right mood for Tammy and Ginny to feel romantic. It was his book *Flying Saucers, Serious Business*, and the magazine article on Betty and Barney Hill getting kidnapped by aliens, and a newspaper clipping on the Mothman.

"How's all this gonna get them romantic?" Patrick asked, pretending to care. He wanted to tell Rex the awful secret, but Rex was so fond of re-telling hidden truths he probably would have told his mom and then it would have gotten back to Patrick's mom.

"Don't you know anything?"

"I don't know *what* I know anymore."

"Don't give up. We're almost there. Look, all we have to do is talk about this stuff and take them for a walk in the cemetery."

"Oh, no, I'm not going to a cemetery."

Rex argued that the cemetery would make kissing them as easy as burning ants with a magnifying glass. He described the moonlight on the graves and Ginny's lips and gave it a pretty good closing argument, but Patrick was too much in awe of death to go near a cemetery. Shadowy acres of tombstones of people who lived and died, moss creeping up over their names, fields of buried bones, regret and ruin with souls under mud, jealous of the living. Mean spirits, invisible enemies, ghost eyes watching as you walk through their prison where they can never get out, and you're just coming and going. Tree limbs could come crashing down, or sinkholes might suck you in, unseen hands dragging you into ten million years of destruction that's only the first page of a story as thick as the phone book. No, sir, he knew too much about death now to risk a cemetery.

"Don't be afraid," Rex said.

"I can't."

Just then there was a knock at the door, and it swung open. It was Rex's mom, holding a drink in one hand and a piece of paper in the other.

"What are you boys doing?"

"Nothing," Rex said.

"Well, don't waste your life away up here. The vacation's almost over." She took a sip of her drink and slinked around the room looking for something.

"What you looking for?"

"Oh, nothing. I'm just missing something, thought maybe Clyde got it. You seen Clyde chewing anything *unusual*?"

"No, what?"

She took another gulp and whirled around toward the door. "Never mind."

Patrick and Rex looked at each other. It was the yellow wig. She was probably working up to another home run and couldn't find it. Last time they saw it was the night outside the theatre when Mr. Jawthorne swiped it off Patrick's head and they ran off so fast. It landed on the sidewalk, and bikers trampled all over it to go see *Easy Rider*.

"Where is Clyde?" she said, stopping by the door and turning around.

"I don't know. He's around, I guess," Rex said.

"Well, don't guess too long. Girl across the way lost her dog." Rex's mom held up the cold drink to her forehead and read the flyer. "She came by today and dropped off this."

Rex stood up, ready to bolt downstairs. "Is she here?"

"No, no, this was before. You were at the beach."

The boys looked at it. It said LOST DOG and had a picture of Sandy, the one the girl from Indiana was always kissing.

"Poor girl. She was almost to tears. I told her, 'Don't worry, honey, he'll come back.' But I don't know. Just don't let Clyde get away. You know your father. If it's time to go, he'll leave without him." She turned off the bedroom light. "What are you boys up to tonight, anyway?"

"Nothing," Rex said.

"Well, get out of here. Why don't you meet those two Khardomah Lodge girls you've been chasing and make a fire down by the beach?"

"We haven't been chasing nobody," Rex said.

"I know what goes on. Make a fire while you still can. You know what those pamphlets they give out at the Chamber of Commerce say?"

"No, what?" Patrick said.

She finished her drink and winked at him. "Grand Haven is for lovers."

# - chapter twenty-six -

THEY GATHERED THE WOOD behind the cottage where Rex hid the minibike. He asked Patrick if he had any money, and he stupidly said yes. Rex knew how to spend Patrick's money better than any friend he'd ever had. They dumped the sticks and bigger limbs in a pile, and Rex said they should zip into town on the minibike to get some gum to have fresh breath for Tammy and Ginny. The minibike engine turned over rough from resting in the damp woods a few days. It coughed like a granddad clearing out phlegm after a nap. Patrick got on first and grabbed the handlebars.

"Hey, get in back, I'm driving," Rex said.

"Hell, no, *you* get in back," Patrick said. "I'm paying for the gum."

Rex gave in, and away they went racing down the hill past the State Park Pavilion. The sunset was coming along orange behind the lighthouse, and people were walking into town, holding hands, and looking shampooed and clean again after a day at the beach. It was the best Patrick had felt all day. The wind was in his face. The bike was under his power. He had cussed out Rex and won an argument. Maybe someday, if the future allowed, Patrick thought he could get a motorcycle and ride around the country with some girl hanging on back.

"Slow down. If you crash, we'll lose our deposit," Rex shouted.

Patrick went even faster.

They got off in front of Steiner's Drug Store and went in for the gum. Rex picked out the biggest pack of Wrigley's Spearmint he could find, which he said was the best gum for kissing. Then when Rex saw Patrick had a couple dollars in his wallet, he looked at his watch and said they had time to do some quick planning at the soda fountain.

"Haven't you got any money?" Patrick said.

"Sorry, left my wallet at the cottage."

They sat on a couple swivel stools, and the lady behind the counter looked at them like they had better not order anything big, because it was almost closing time. She picked up a half-empty Coke glass from the last guy and wiped the sweat ring off the counter.

"You decided yet?" she asked.

Rex ordered a Zombie, which Patrick had never heard of. The waitress hadn't either. She was a town woman who wanted to get home with her family and change her shoes. Rex gave her the recipe on how to make a Zombie in the voice of a teacher telling a kindergartner about algebra.

"You take a glass and put in a little chocolate syrup at the bottom."

"Yes."

"Then you give it a shot of 7 Up."

"Yes."

"Then add a little Dr. Pepper."

"OK."

"And then a little Coke and Pepsi and some cherry syrup."

"Is that all?"

"Maybe a little root beer, but be careful to keep it all even."

"OK, what do you want?" she said turning to Patrick.

"I'll have a cherry Coke, please."

"Right."

"One more thing, let me borrow your pen," Rex said.

She flipped her pen on the counter and went to work, and Rex got out a napkin from the curved-top, chrome napkin dispenser to sketch out his plans for the bonfire make out. He drew a bird's eye view of the beach down south of the Bil-Mar motel and Pirates Cove restaurant where the shore rose up into small dunes and tall grass. He spent a lot of time inking in the grass, which Patrick told him was a waste of time, but Rex had to get everything right.

"The grass will give us privacy," he said. "We'll build the fire here so nobody around will see it, and we can be all alone with Tammy and Ginny."

"Then what?"

"I brought along this article for you to study."

"What article?"

He pulled out the newspaper clipping from his shirt pocket on the Mothman. Patrick remembered the A&W incident and looked over his shoulder to see who was behind them. Nobody.

"Here you go," the waitress said, bringing their drinks.

"Thanks," Patrick said. But Rex said nothing. He took his glass to taste it first, to see if she followed his orders. She pretended the counter needed another swipe with her wet rag while she waited to see if Rex was pleased. He put the straw to his lips and sucked the dark potion into his mouth.

"Excellent! We'll give you a little something extra in your tip," he said.

The lady smiled and walked away to a sink of gray water and dirty dishes that were waiting.

"*A little something extra?* That's *my* money you're giving away."

"Shhhhh … I know," Rex whispered, "but these town people work all summer while the tourists have fun. You can't just think of yourself all the time."

Patrick saw a sign behind the counter for Dad's Root Beer and thought about his own dad. How much time would he have? Another year? Six months? Would he soon be lying in a hospital bed saying goodbye to everybody? It was wrong to even want to kiss a girl with his dad facing death. But the project gave him something else to think about. Patrick took some feeble sips of his cherry Coke and reviewed the Mothman article while Rex sucked the Zombie through his straw.

"Tonight's the night," Rex said.

"I don't know."

"What do you mean you don't know?"

"What does Mothman have to do with all this?" Patrick said, tapping the napkin map.

"Don't you remember?"

"What?"

"The time we were playing pinball, and I told Tammy and Ginny about the aliens attacking the astronauts on the way to the moon?"

"I remember."

"When I told them how the aliens might attack the astronauts, Tammy said she was scared of that stuff and put her hand on my shoulder!"

"Yeah."

"And in that Jerry Lewis movie, when it got exciting, Ginny reached over and grabbed my hand?"

Patrick drank his cherry Coke and looked at the Mothman article. He could see what Rex was getting at. Just scare the girls, and they'll lean all over the nearest boy, easy to kiss. It seemed like a lot of work and a tricky thing to pull on two girls from Atlanta who probably never heard of Mothman or the bridge falling in the river killing those forty-six people.

"You ever really have a feeling for a girl, Rex?"

"Sure, every girl, if she's good-looking."

"No, I mean a girl you have that feeling for all around. Some girl at school, maybe? You notice her one day, and for no reason, you just get that *new feeling* you've never had before, and you want to know everything about her and start to care about her. I guess that's what it means to like a girl *as a person*."

*"As a person?"*

"Yeah, as a person."

"What are you talking about? It's Thursday night. We gotta get moving!"

"I know, I know. I just thought maybe we should come up with some questions for Tammy and Ginny to get to know them as persons."

Rex shook his head, slurping off the last of his Zombie loud and determined. "Look, just read up on Mothman for backup," Rex said. "I'll talk first about the UFOs and the way they come up out of the lake at night from their bases looking for people to do kidnappings on. That should be enough. But if they need a little more push, I'll say, *Hey, Patrick, what about the Mothman?*"

"OK, but how will we know when to kiss them, I mean, the exact moment?" Patrick asked.

Rex looked at the napkin map and gave it some thought. "You're right. We need a code word."

"A code word?"

"You know, a signal that when one of us says that word, it's bombs away, time to start kissing no matter what."

"Well, what if Ginny's head's turned the wrong way?"

Rex started chewing on his ice impatiently. "Just kiss her on the cheek and then swoop over for her lips like your brother did with that town girl."

"OK."

"We need a code word, now. Think. You know any good code words?"

"I know one," Patrick said.

"What is it?"

"*Hick*-tah-minnicka-hannicka-sock-tah-*boom*-tah-*lay* ... *Yoo hoo!*"

*"Hick-tah-what?"*

"*Hick*-tah-minnicka-hannicka-sock-tah-*boom*-tah-*lay* ... *Yoo hoo!*"

"That's too long," Rex said. "How about Alfred E. Neuman?"

"Fine. Alfred E. Neuman means bombs away."

"Here's your bill," the waitress said. It was twenty-five cents for the cherry Coke and fifty for Rex's Zombie, plus tax.

"Give her a dollar tip," Rex said loud enough for the waitress to hear. "Treat her like a person."

Patrick paid for the sodas, the dollar tip, and the gum, and put the article on Mothman in his shirt pocket for later. They went outside, and it was fresh dark. The voice of the Musical Fountain man was echoing from the harbor down Washington Avenue, welcoming people to another night of enjoyment. Patrick looked around and wished his dad would come out of nowhere like he had the night outside the theatre, saying you have to come home and spend the night with the family. But he wasn't there. Rex revved up the minibike, and they hurried back to his cottage to walk over to the Khardomah Lodge and get the girls.

# - chapter twenty-seven -

TAMMY AND GINNY sat on the front porch swing of the Khardomah Lodge rocking back and forth under a milk glass light with moths swirling around, while Patrick and Rex hid in some bushes across the street. The porch swing creaked like a metronome at a piano lesson, while the girls voices played a duet of high notes to each other, chatting away about something the boys couldn't hear. They started to sneak toward the porch but then saw Mr. Jawthorne sitting near the girls, reading a newspaper and chewing on an unlit cigar. He didn't see the boys. Cars drove by, and other guests came and went out the front screen door while Mr. Jawthorne looked the paper up and down ,studying business conditions that might affect his trucking company. Everyone was on the go, except Patrick and Rex. They were stuck in the bushes waiting. Finally Mr. Jawthorne stretched and looked over at his prisoners.

"Girls, the paper says it's so hot back home, people are dying. That's the only reason I take my family into this Yankee stronghold. It's cool."

Then he went back to reading while the girls kept swinging. When Rex saw Mr. Jawthorne's face was behind the newspaper, he waved to get the girls' attention. They were looking out for the boys' signal because Rex had body surfed with them on the beach and made the date.

"Daddy, we want to do something," Tammy said, swinging next to Ginny.

"Well, read a book or play pinball."

"We want to go *out*."

"Out? There's nothing out there in the world that you can't enjoy here where it's safe."

"Down at the Bil-Mar, in the lobby, they got a bowling machine. We want to walk down there and put a quarter in."

"It's dark. You can't be out after dark."

"Oh, let the girls have some fun," said Mrs. Jawthorne, swinging open the screen door and stretching her arm up the doorframe. She wore a pretty dress with flowers on it, and her figure showed in the light from the lobby behind her. Mr. Jawthorne looked up and noticed her. She moved out into the night air to sit down beside him. Her love seat landing messed up the newspaper, and Mr. Jawthorne had to refold the entire business section to get things right.

"Clarissa! What are you saying?"

"Don't you remember when you were their age and the night breeze called and you wanted to have a little fun after dark?"

"I remember what happened the other night ... at the theatre."

"I know, I know," she said, fingering the hair behind his ears, "But they aren't going into town. Just down the hill to play a little bowling at the Bil-Mar. Let them stretch their legs so you and I can … talk."

Patrick and Rex looked at each other.

"Well, all right, but no boys. And look both ways before you cross the street."

Tammy and Ginny leaped off the porch swing and ran down the sidewalk past the bushes where the boys were hiding. Patrick and Rex stayed hidden. When the girls were out of sight, Mrs. Jawthorne threw her husband's cigar in the ivy and covered his face with hers. The boys got up and ran for the girls.

Lake Michigan was playing a love song of soft waves when the boys plunked down the firewood about fifty feet from shore in a little nook of a dune surrounded by knee-high privacy grass. Rex stuffed the ripped-up pages of his dad's stock market newspaper in the wood and struck matches to get it going. The fire was eager. It spread to the little sticks fast, then fed on the bigger sticks and licked on the logs. The girls flung out two beach towels Rex had rolled up, one for each couple. Soon the fire was warm and popping on its own. The boys sat down next to their dates, the exact way Rex had mapped it out on the napkin. The lake was dark and mysterious, reflecting the red beacon on the lighthouse pulsing like a lonely heartbeat.

"It's hard to believe mankind is up there right now," Rex said looking overhead at the moon.

"Who?" Tammy said looking up.

"I mean the astronauts up there pushing through the night getting closer and closer to the moon."

"Yeah," Tammy said. "I'm glad we're here where it's safe."

"I feel sorry for them not having any high-caliber weapons on board," Rex said, "to protect themselves."

"You got any gum?" Ginny said.

"Sure, here," Rex said. He got the Jumbo pack of Wrigley's Spearmint out and gave everybody one. They were all quiet, chewing their gum and looking at the stars. Ginny gave off a minty breath shiver, so Patrick whipped off his windbreaker and put it over her shoulders to keep her warm.

"Thank you," she said, giving Patrick a tender glance.

"Up there in space, it's a whole different set of rules," Rex said.

"You talk like you know everything. What rules?" Tammy said.

"The space rules. Different groups from different planets flying around; they might treat the astronauts like they treated Betty and Barney Hill."

"Like who?" Ginny said.

Rex had them going. They leaned forward to listen while he poked the fire with a stick and the flames reflected on his face. The waves were swishing in rhythm like a clock down the hallway in the middle of the night when it's too scary to get up and go to the bathroom. He told how Betty and Barney got kidnapped on a dark road after they noticed a bright light following their car.

"That's bullshit," Tammy said.

"What if it's true?" Ginny said.

"You take Lake Michigan here. I've read the aliens have underwater stations where they park their ships to hide from view, and then at night...."

Ginny's hand scooped in around Patrick's left arm. He could feel her fingertips grip his leaf-raking muscles as she leaned into his shoulder.

"There are strange lights seen all the time coming up out of the lake, and nobody knows what they are or who's driving them. They may be flying up and down the lake looking for fresh people to steal," Rex said.

"Don't talk no more," Tammy said. "Let's just hold each other and look at the fire. Tonight, I want to feel like Cinderella. Only I don't want the clock to chime midnight. The vacation is almost over. Soon we'll go back home and go back to school in the fall and probably never see each other again our whole lives."

"That's so sad," Ginny said, shrugging into Patrick.

"I just wonder if anybody will ever kiss me before I die," Tammy said.

Rex tossed his stick in the fire and looked at Tammy. Tammy looked at Ginny. Ginny looked at Patrick.

"I need some ChapStick," Ginny said, stretching.

"Me, too," Tammy said. "Have you got any?"

"Yeah, hold on," Ginny said, reaching around and digging in her pocket. Patrick and Rex were in absolute silence, like kids on the top of the stairs before the parents say it's OK to come down on Christmas morning.

"Here it is," Ginny said. She uncapped it and smeared some on her lips. The ChapStick smell was near enough to taste. Then she handed it to Patrick. He never used ChapStick, but tonight he put some on, too. With the cap in one hand, he twisted out more ChapStick and reached over to give it to Tammy.

"Here you go."

The ChapStick dispenser was a little greasy. His fingers trembled. He dropped it.

"Shit, you dropped it!" Tammy said. "You'll get sand all over it now."

"Don't worry, don't worry." Rex sprang up. "I'll find it. We'll clean it off."

Patrick and Rex both thrashed around in the sand looking for it. Rex found it.

"Here it is," he said, picking off sand particles. "Good as new." He held it out to Tammy, but she was looking at the lake.

"Wait a minute, what's that?" she said.

They all looked. A white light shined over the horizon above the water.

"What's wrong?" Ginny said.

"That light. It just blinked on out of nowhere."

Rex looked again. "That light? It's just a star. Here, have some ChapStick, Tammy."

She pushed away his hand. "No, look. It's bigger than a star. And besides, it looked like it just *popped up* … out of the water."

"That's not possible. Let's all sit back down and relax," Rex said.

"I don't want to relax," Tammy said. She was studying the light. She and Ginny both were standing close to the campfire watching the light. Rex looked at Patrick and shook his head.

"Hey, girls," Rex said. "Let's all sit down. Patrick wants to tell us something."

"Tell us what?" Tammy said.

"Yeah, what?" Ginny said.

They both looked at Patrick, hoping for some good news.

He took a deep breath. "Well, a few years back in West Virginia, on a dark night…."

"We don't give a shit about West Virginia. Look at that light," Tammy said.

"No, listen. He's gonna tell us about Mothman," Rex said. "That light's nothing but a plane."

"Shut up," Tammy said, punching Rex's shoulder like a prizefighter, "You yourself said they come up out of the lake. I'm telling you it came up out of the lake."

"Maybe it's just a plane that came up over the horizon and *looked* like it came out of the lake," Rex said, rubbing his shoulder. "Please, let's sit down."

They all sat down, with the girls snuggled next to each other in the middle while Patrick and Rex manned the bookends by their dates.

"I think it's getting closer," Tammy said. "It's getting bigger, and it's getting closer."

They all studied it.

"You're right; it is getting bigger," Ginny gasped.

"Maybe it sees the campfire, and they're using it as a guide to come snatch us," Tammy said.

"That's not possible," Rex said in a soft, romantic voice. "It's just a plane; don't worry. Alfred E. Neuman never worries."

THIS WAS IT. The code word was spoken. Rex shot a glance behind the girls' backs at Patrick. It was time to lean in for the cheek kiss, then drift over into the lip kiss. Patrick looked at Ginny's cheek as she stared forward at the mystery light. Her profile glowed like the face of the moon, and his lips were the lunar module on final approach. Five, four, three, two … closing his eyes, Patrick leaned his lips toward the vast unknown. Rex was doing the same thing on the opposite side with Tammy.

"THEY'RE USING THE FIRE TO ZERO IN ON US!" Ginny shouted, lurching forward, dragging her hair across Patrick's lips.

"SHIT! PUT OUT THE FIRE. WE HAVE TO PUT OUT THE FIRE!" Tammy yelled, bonking foreheads with Rex.

"HURRY UP!" Ginny yelled.

Tammy and Ginny shoved away the boys and threw fistfuls of sand at the fire. Patrick and Rex started kicking sand on the fire to please them, but then they, too, saw the UFO was coming right for them, so they worked all the harder to put out the fire.

"I want my daddy!" Tammy whimpered. "They're coming for us!"

Tammy and Ginny ran up the dune, leaving Patrick and Rex kicking sand on the flames in a panic. A spotlight shone on them as they dove into the privacy grass. Smoke stung and sand swirled in Patrick's eyes as the craft passed right overhead with a loud noise and disappeared inland.

"What was it?" Patrick panted.

"Idiots!"

"What was it?"

"Coast Guard helicopter." Rex rubbed his forehead. "They must've been using our campfire for rescue practice."

The boys ran to catch the girls, finding Patrick's jacket abandoned on the road. They ran as fast as they could. But the girls beat them back to the Khardomah Lodge before they could tell them everything was OK. They saw the girls on the porch under the moth lights talking with Mr. Jawthorne, moving their arms around, and decided to leave them alone until Friday morning. They didn't know it then, but that's when Mr. Jawthorne would come riding for revenge.

# - chapter twenty-eight -

PATRICK AND REX SAT despairing in Rex's cottage living room the next morning. Suddenly, it was Friday. Rex was spying out the window with his binoculars for the girl from Indiana while Patrick apologized for his poor workmanship on the project the night before. He had sneaked away from his own family for a quick check on things, because after breakfast Dad had warned the boys not to cut loose to the four winds today. It was the last day of the trip, a day for laundry and dishes, a day for sweeping and vacuuming, a day for packing suitcases to put on the top of the car. He gave a big speech about it. After breakfast Dad took John and Teddy with him into town to get rope for the car, and tape and cardboard to protect his antique pictures from breaking. That left Mom, Elizabeth, baby Joey, and Patrick to stick around. Mom was having a bad back and sat down to watch *I Love Lucy* on the rental TV. She dozed off while Lucy was pretending to be Superman for little Rickie's birthday party. Lucy got stuck on the ledge, and the real Superman had to come and rescue her. Elizabeth and baby Joey were watching TV with her, so when Mom fell asleep, Patrick whispered to Elizabeth that he was just going down the block to the red cottage and would be right back.

"If only you hadn't dropped the ChapStick!" Rex said.

"I know. I know."

"Our only chance now, since the trip is almost over is the goodbye kiss."

"The goodbye kiss?"

"Yes, it's all we have left. But if we time it just right—"

Just then, Rex's mom came in the living room with a cup of coffee and sat down.

"Rex, are you still spying for that Indiana girl with those binoculars?"

"No, what? What are you talking about?"

"That window doesn't point at the lake. You leave that poor girl alone."

"Did she find her dog?" Patrick said.

"No, I hope she does. I heard the story on that dog," she said with an intriguing hint of concern.

"Let's go outside and ride the minibike," Rex said, starting to walk away.

"Don't you want to know, Rex?" his mom called after him.

He kept walking and didn't answer. But Patrick wanted to know all about her. "What story?" he said.

Rex stopped by the edge of the living room with his back to them.

Rex's mom lowered her voice. "That poor girl lost her father this winter to cancer. Last summer he was alive, and this summer…."

"That fast?"

"That fast. Her mother told me yesterday. Don't repeat this," she whispered, "but her father bought her that dog last summer in Grand Haven as a puppy. She's been sad all week missing her father, and now the dog is gone, too. That dog was the last happy connection she had with him."

Patrick looked over at Rex. He signaled for Patrick to come on. They went outside, and it was windy.

"Look," Rex said. "The weather is changing."

Down on the beach big waves were crashing in. The sky out over the lake was cloudy, and the lifeguard had taken down the yellow flag and put up a red one.

"That's so sad about that girl," Patrick said.

"Yeah." He sat on the minibike and started the engine.

"It must be a terrible thing to lose your dad."

"Yeah."

"Where's your dad?"

"I don't know. Probably golfing. You want to go for a ride?"

"No, I have to get back to the cottage."

"Come on."

Rex's mom came out, wincing at the weather, sipping her coffee. "Rex, I want you to take that minibike back to the rental shop before this weather hits."

"But Mom, we've got all day."

"Son, it's the last day. Do it now, so your father won't get mad."

Right then, Rex saw something that his mom and Patrick didn't, something that made him obey right away. It was Mr. Jawthorne with cigar in mouth coming right for them.

"I'll return it right now," Rex said, driving off.

Rex's mom turned to go inside. Patrick started to walk across the sandy yard when he saw him. Mr. Jawthorne, his face as red as the cottage, was closing in like a cannonball flying straight for its mark. But at that same second, Patrick saw his sister, Elizabeth, running straight for him.

"Boy, don't you run!" Mr. Jawthorne yelled. "We are going to have it out!"

Rex's mom heard the yelling and turned around to look.

Mr. Jawthorne grabbed Patrick's shirt. Patrick met his eyes, then looked over at Elizabeth coming from his left and Rex's mom coming from his right.

"Patrick! She's having the baby!" Elizabeth cried out.

They all looked at Elizabeth. Mr. Jawthorne let go of Patrick.

*"Having the baby?"* Mr. Jawthorne and Rex's mom said it together.

Rex's mom bent her knees to get down on Elizabeth's eye level. "Is your daddy taking her to the hospital?"

Elizabeth put her fingers in her mouth and sucked them. Patrick told Rex's mom that Dad went into town to get rope.

"Oh my gosh, my husband's out golfing with our car," Rex's mom said, turning to Mr. Jawthorne. "Can you drive her?"

Mr. Jawthorne looked back toward the Khardomah Lodge, then remembered. "No, my wife took the car to shop for shoes."

"Did your mommy call an ambulance?" Rex's mom asked Elizabeth.

Elizabeth didn't know what an ambulance was. So Patrick reminded Rex's mom that they didn't even have a telephone at the cottage.

"I'll call one right away!" she said, running inside.

Elizabeth turned and ran back toward the cottage. Patrick chased after her. Mr. Jawthorne chased after Patrick. Halfway, Mr. Jawthorne and Patrick held Elizabeth's hands and all three ran together. With her little legs, she was slowing them down, so Mr. Jawthorne scooped her up under his arm like a pet pig, and they sprinted the final stretch. The screen door banged open against the refrigerator, as Patrick slid into the kitchen and fell in a puddle of Mom's broken water she had splashed out a few minutes earlier.

"Over here!" Mom yelled.

Mr. Jawthorne put down Elizabeth next to Patrick. "You watch your sister and stay out of the way. Y'hear?"

"Yes, sir."

"And here, *hold this*." He handed Patrick his unlit cigar and dashed into the living room.

"Thank God; are you a doctor?" Mom asked.

"No, ma'am, I own Jawthorne Trucking."

"Mr. Jawthorne? Do you even know what you're doing?"

"Ma'am, the Jawthornes always know what they're doing when a woman is in peril. Ambulance is coming, but I'll need to take a look just in case."

There were some scuffling noises, and Patrick heard Mom groaning, and then Mr. Jawthorne yelled to Patrick, "Boy, you go get me some towels and then stay out of my way." Then he turned back to Mom, and said all reassuring, "OK, ma'am, you're gonna be jus' fine. Now do exactly what I say and *push*!"

Patrick ran to the bathroom and got some beach towels, then gave them to Mr. Jawthorne before retreating back into the corner with Elizabeth. It was some tense going with Mom grunting and moaning. Elizabeth held onto Patrick's pants leg while they peeked around the corner from the kitchen. They could see Mom's legs open, with Mr. Jawthorne squatted down like a catcher. Baby Joey was in the living room only a few feet away, still watching the rental TV. On the screen, muscle man Jack LaLanne was counting off ninety-nine jumping jacks while his German Shepherd dog, Happy, barked.

"Seventy-four, seventy-five, seventy-six...."

"Don't let up now! Take the fort!" Mr. Jawthorne urged.

Mom pushed some more. Jack LaLanne counted more jumping jacks. "Eighty-two, eighty-three, eighty-four...." Happy kept barking, and Patrick and Elizabeth saw a head coming out. Patrick was so nervous, he put Mr. Jawthorne's cigar in his mouth. It had a sharp bite at first, but no worse than a lady cigar on the train tracks back home. He began drawing on it, wishing it were lit.

"Here we go. We're breaking through enemy lines!" Mr. Jawthorne cried.

Mom let out a long, satisfied sigh. And Jawthorne jiggled the slippery baby in his hands, unwrapping the cord from around its neck.

"A girl child is born!" he announced big as the whole outdoors.

The baby started crying, a squeaky, sad little cry, and he handed her to Mom, who held her on her blouse. Elizabeth ran in to see. Patrick heard the siren from the approaching ambulance and went immediately to the stove and turned up the blue gas flame all the way to light the cigar. It roared to life and delivered a powerful cloud of calmness. So much so that Patrick ducked outside to have a few more puffs. It had been a whole week since he had smoked, and now he was feeling like himself again.

"Is she all right? Is she all right?" Rex's mom ran up to Patrick, waving the ambulance in.

"It's a girl," he nodded, puffing.

Rex's mom and the ambulance team trotted in as Mr. Jawthorne came out. He was wiping his hands with a dish towel, which he threw at Patrick to catch, then took back his cigar.

"A man's cigar is a man's cigar!" He planted it between his lips and puffed a bit. "And same goes for a man's daughter. How old are you?"

"Eleven."

"Eleven?"

"When I was your age," he started in a high tone, studying Patrick. Then he thought about a kiss he stole from a girl way back then. It had been a moonlit night on a vacation in Ft. Lauderdale, and he could still remember how she closed her eyes and tilted her face up toward his just so.

"Yes?" Patrick asked.

His voice softened. "Well, I guess I was the same way." He was quiet for a few puffs, thinking, then ruled on the matter, decisive like a Jawthorne man should be. "Maybe you're *me* I've been chasing off all along. Maybe we're all a bit like Sherman's raiders."

"What?"

He gave Patrick the rest of his cigar without explaining and walked away. Patrick studied Mr. Jawthorne's figure as he disappeared into the distance, and Patrick smoked up the cigar good and hot. When the ambulance crew came out, wheeling Mom and the new baby, he tossed the cigar in a bush. Rex's mom followed them out with baby Joey in one arm and Elizabeth in the other. Mom looked over at Patrick.

"Tell your father I'm fine," she said. "And the baby's fine, too."

Patrick and Rex's mom waved goodbye as the ambulance drove away. Rex's mom turned to Patrick.

"Your mom asked me to watch these two little ones at our place. You stay here and tell your Dad the good news when he gets back. OK?"

"OK."

"Where's Mr. Jawthorne?"

"Oh, he left."

"What a surprising man."

"Yeah."

When Rex's mom got far enough down the road, Patrick ran for the cigar to have a few more puffs. It was nourishing to him after all the excitement. Then he tossed it far away and went inside and got a Pepsi out of the refrigerator and sat down on the couch. Jack LaLanne was still exercising on the TV, and Betsy Wetsy lay on the rug, not far from where the real baby was born. When Dad came in with John and Teddy, Patrick told them the news. Dad dropped the luggage rope and ran back out the door, then stopped and told the boys to stick together and stay in the cottage. "Boys, this is great news. Whatever you do, don't go to the beach."

# - chapter twenty-nine -

THE BEACH WAS WINDY when they got there. Rex made them go. John, Patrick and Teddy had been sitting around the cottage being obedient, doing nothing, when Rex ran in the kitchen. He knew all about the new baby. To celebrate, he said, they should go down to the beach. "Not supposed to? Come on, it's the last day," he said. "You have to live on vacation before it's over." On and on he went, until he wore them down. They weren't that hard to wear down. Really, the whole week had slipped by, and they hadn't had one red flag day except the one they missed by antiquing. Through the cottage window they could see the white caps and brave swimmers having fun. Swimming was forbidden on red flag days. A gap in the sandbar could open up, and the riptide would pull swimmers out to drown like dirt down a bathtub drain. But all the happiest kids swam on red flag days, and no lifeguard tried to stop them.

Rex's parents had also forbidden swimming on red flag days, and he'd promised he wouldn't. But when he got to Patrick's cottage, he stripped off his clothes and threw them on the couch. Underneath was his swimming suit. John, Patrick, and Teddy hopped into their suits, laughing and figuring they had about an hour to sneak a swim and get back in time to dry their hair before Dad would get back from the hospital.

"Come on, we're missing all the fun," Rex said.

At the beach, they laid out their towels and kicked off their shoes to go in the lake. Hardly anyone was there, because it too cloudy to sunbathe. The metal detector man had the sand all to himself, surveying a windswept beach without footprints where yesterday's lost quarters or gold earrings lay hidden, ready to be discovered. Up and down the shoreline, it was mostly teenagers in the water, guys whose voices had changed, and their shouts and laughter were deep. The four boys ran in. The water was cold at first, but after they went under, they got used to it and the wind felt warm on their skin. Four-foot-tall waves rose up—a hill of water coming right at them, pushed by the gust front of a thunderstorm moving in from the horizon. They'd jump in front of a big wave and then rocket in about thirty feet until their stomachs scraped along the sandy bottom as the water shoved them toward the shore. Then they staggered to their feet, coughing up water, laughing, and ready to do it all over again.

Patrick thought it was good not to have to worry about Tammy and Ginny for a change. This was much easier than trying to kiss a girl. The boys would ride one wave in and then walk out to catch another. Crashing in at an angle, the waves edged them farther and farther down the beach. After about a half hour, they noticed they were down by the Bil-Mar, and their towels were way up shore. So they got out, all four of them safe, and walked up shore to get back to their towels. The approaching storm was getting closer.

"That was some fish you almost caught the other night," Rex said to Teddy.

"Yeah, but he got away."

"At least you had him for a little while," Rex said.

"I guess."

"You're one of the big kids now," Rex said.

"Really?"

"Sure."

Rex was working up to something with Teddy, but nobody knew what yet.

"We should be heading back soon," John said.

"Hell, we just got here," Rex said.

"I know, but we had our fun. Let's go before it rains," John said.

"No, wait, look out there," Rex said. He stopped walking and pointed way up beach at the pier.

Giant waves were crashing into the concrete and splashing big white clouds of water onto stick people way out by the fog house.

"Are there people out there?" Teddy asked.

"They must be having real fun," Rex said.

"They're fools," Patrick said.

"Then we should be fools, too," Rex argued.

"No way," John said. "We can't go out on the pier. It's gonna storm. It's too dangerous."

"I guess you're right," Rex said.

They gathered up their towels to leave.

"Uh-oh, you hear that?" Rex said.

"What?" John asked.

"I thought I heard a school bell," Rex said.

"There's no school bell," Patrick said. "That's weeks away."

"Yeah, I know. But I thought I heard it. Are you looking forward to school?" Rex asked Teddy.

"No."

"Are you?" he said turning to John and Patrick.

"No," they said.

Rex turned back to the pier. "Just look at that. Do you want to be sitting in your desk in a few months, doing math or history, and think back to this very moment and say you wished you had gone?"

They were all quiet and reverent at the question, so Rex answered for them.

"Hell, let's have all the fun we can before school starts."

Rex threw down his towel and started to run for the pier. They dropped their towels and ran after him.

When their bare feet reached the pier—that twelve-hundred-foot-long pretense of safety in a raging lake—the storm was just minutes away. A wall of black and purple clouds churned over the horizon moving toward them fast. The gusts whipped up ten-foot-tall waves that rushed along the teeth-shaped hem of the pier, bursting spray from tip to shore, looking for legs to grab. Rex wanted to go all the way out, but he kept that to himself.

"Hold onto the catwalk!" Rex shouted, leading the way.

"Far enough," John said as they got to the halfway point beside the lighthouse. He was speaking in his own voice now, no British accent, because he was scared. They were all scared. They rested by the love graffiti and looked down pier to see what was coming. A dozen or so kids were running toward them, their feet slapping on the wet pavement. Storm refugees. Fleeing kids ran past the lighthouse and kept running for shore.

"Come on. We have to say we did it," Rex said.

"No way! Everybody's leaving," Patrick said.

Rex nodded like he agreed, then bolted on ahead without looking back, just as the rain starting pelting the pier. John and Patrick were watching Rex, ready to turn back, when suddenly Teddy got brave and ran after Rex.

"Hey, Teddy, wait!"

John and Patrick shrugged at each other and ran to keep up. The rain and wind raged even stronger, and lightning flashed close to the pier. Pleasure boats trying to beat the devil raced down the Grand River while the boys went farther out. They hung onto the iron supports of the catwalk as each wave hit. The waves washing over the pier shot between their legs ankle deep. And the wind, ripping around them, forced them to shout louder to be heard.

"WE CAN'T GO OUT ANY FARTHER!" Patrick yelled to Rex as they held onto a catwalk strut together.

"IT WASN'T BECAUSE YOU DROPPED THE CHAPSTICK."

"WHAT?"

"WE WERE SCARED."

"WHAT ARE YOU TALKING ABOUT?"

"THAT'S WHY WE COULDN'T KISS THEM."

"YOU'RE CRAZY. THIS IS IT, NO FARTHER," Patrick shouted, grabbing Rex's arm.

"IF WE GO TO THE END, WE WON'T BE AFRAID TO KISS THEM GOODBYE." Rex pulled his arm free and kept going.

Patrick stood there thinking about Ginny's lips, as John and Teddy ran to his side.

"WHAT DID HE SAY?" John yelled.

"HE SAID WE HAVE TO KEEP GOING!" Patrick ran on between wave hits toward the fog house. Following Rex, he took the Grand River side, the safer side, where the current was softer and they could walk the final stretch on a concrete ledge higher off the water. Rex and Patrick rounded the corner to the front tip of the fog house where a group of teenaged boys with muscles stood, shirtless and shivering. Patrick could tell by the way they talked, their confidence and stretched-out vowels, that they were town guys who knew the lake. It was several members of the Grand Haven high school football team. The Buccaneers would go on to have an impressive 8-1 record this coming season. Their coach would later think he alone had instilled them with unity and tenacity, but it was really the lake that day that bound them together. John and Teddy reached the group, and they all stood there catching their breath.

"GO NOW!" one of the teens yelled.

A Buccaneer defensive lineman, beefy and sure, ran as fast as he could on the final apron of concrete to the very tip of the pier with just seconds to go before a twelve-foot wave came on him. He squatted down around a yellow, mushroom-shaped metal post for tying off boats.

"HANG ON!" the teenagers yelled. The lineman hugged the boat tie like a fumbled football. Patrick felt arms whip over his chest the way Dad would guard him when he slammed on the brakes in the car. Strangers' hands pushed against his ribs, and his against theirs, a team of boys knit together by arms with their backs against the cowcatcher-shaped concrete wall of the fog house. The wave landed furiously, swallowing the lineman, and licking over the rest of them like a lake monster hungry for boys.

"SHITTTTTTTTT!!!!!!" everyone yelled.

The wave fell back and everyone blinked to see if the Buccaneer on the boat tie was still alive. He let go and ran back to the group with everyone laughing.

"LET'S GO BACK NOW!" John shouted.

Before they could go, Rex ran out and held onto the boat tie. They all braced for another hit and the lake came down on Rex.

The after-spray hit them even harder than the first time, a firing squad of watery BB's stinging their bare skin. Patrick realized Rex was dead. He kept his eyes shut, not wanting to open them and see the empty boat tie. Patrick heard the football team cheering and looked. Rex was wobbling back to safety. He jabbed Patrick in the stomach.

"PATRICK, MY GOD! YOU HAVE TO DO IT FOR TONIGHT. I SWEAR! AFTER THAT, YOU CAN'T LOSE!"

# - chapter thirty -

REX WAS RIGHT. Patrick shouldn't have done it, but after he did do it, he was a changed person. He knew now that kissing Ginny goodbye was unavoidable. The football players applauded as the four tourist boys ran back in the rain toward the shore where they found their wind-whipped towels and headed back to the cottage. Dad wasn't home yet, so they kicked off their suits, ran around the coffee table naked and laughing and whooping, then put on dry clothes and got out Mom's blow dryer to make sure their hair wasn't wet. Rex dried his hair first and then left for his cottage. John, Patrick, and Teddy took turns blow-drying their hair. Even after that, Dad still wasn't home, so they went to work. They did the dishes, took out the trash, made their beds, packed their suitcases, and sponge-washed the rug where Mom had the baby, then vacuumed and swept. When Dad finally came in the door, carrying a bucket of Kentucky Fried chicken in one hand and baby Joey in the other with Elizabeth tagging along, he smiled big and bright.

"Boys! Good work! I expected to find you watching TV."

"How's the baby?" John said.

"Great! And Elizabeth has a surprise. Tell them her name."

Elizabeth came forward, proud and bashful. "Betsy."

"Betsy? You named her after a doll?" Patrick said.

"It was your mother's idea. She said during the whole delivery she kept seeing that doll on the rug and was thinking, 'Heavens to Betsy!'" Dad laughed at that one like he hadn't laughed all week.

The boys ripped the lid off the chicken bucket and started eating. Dad opened the refrigerator and got out a beer. But before he drank any, he cleared his throat. "Boys, let's say grace before we eat."

They stopped chewing and bowed their heads. They all prayed with him. "In the name of the Father, and the Son, and the Holy Spirit. Bless us, oh Lord, and these thy gifts which we are about to receive from thy bounty through Christ our Lord, Amen." They made the sign of the cross and dug in. Dad drank a few sips of his beer and started laughing again. He was in the best mood of the whole trip.

"What's so funny?" Teddy said.

"Boys, Elizabeth, I have something to tell you." He sat down at the table, and the kids all thought it was news about the new baby. But then he revealed the secret to everyone.

"Before the trip, I had some tests done to find out what was wrong with me, why I was having so many sore throats."

Patrick put down his drumstick.

"I thought I was really sick. But today at the hospital, with the new baby here, I couldn't wait any longer. So I called my doctor long distance in St. Louis to find out the results of the tests."

"What tests?" John said.

"X-rays," Dad said, "to find out if I have cancer."

Cancer! Everybody stopped eating. Even Teddy looked afraid. "You have cancer?" Teddy said.

Dad reached in his pocket and slapped a roll of downtown breath mints on the counter. They all looked at it.

"Doctor says I have inflammation of the esophagus caused by too many of these."

They all looked at the breath mints.

"Are you OK?" John said.

"I'm gonna live," he said holding out his arms.

Everyone got up to hug Dad. When it was his turn, Patrick started to cry. The burden he had carried since he had heard Dad tell Mr. Finley about the X-rays fell from his heart like a boulder. To hide his tears, he kissed Dad on the lips. That made him cry even more, because he hadn't kissed Dad on the lips since Christmas morning 1964, the year he got the Hasbro GI Joe Desert Patrol Jeep Machine Gun. Dad started to cry, too, and laugh, and he tickled Patrick and messed up his hair to get him to laugh. Patrick felt ashamed and had to go to the bathroom to wash his face. Then when he saw his face in the mirror, he cried even more. He slapped himself to grow up, and splashed some cold water on his face. Patrick rubbed it down good with a towel to look like nothing happened so John and Teddy couldn't study him and know he was weak. It was the greatest news of the trip, but he felt like a fool.

"Boys," Dad said as Patrick came back to the table, "after dinner we need to pack the top of the car. We leave tomorrow morning to pick up your Mom and Betsy from the hospital to drive home."

"How are we all gonna fit in the car?" Teddy said.

"Yeah, and with all that junk you bought?" John said.

Dad got up and scratched his head. He hadn't thought of this when he was buying Sherman's March to the Sea and all the other framed pictures.

"Maybe we'll just have to put Teddy in the way back seat with you two big boys."

Teddy was happy to hear that. He always felt he was missing out on the party in the way back seat.

"Dad, before we pack, can I go see Rex real quick?"

"What for?"

"We want to say goodbye to somebody."

"What have you got—a girlfriend up here?" Dad said, laughing.

Everybody laughed at Patrick, but that was OK. That meant he was going to say yes.

# - chapter thirty-one -

PATRICK RAN OVER TO REX'S, feeling happy and confident. Dad was OK, and there was still time to say goodbye to Tammy and Ginny. When he got there, Rex's family was having breakfast for dinner, scrambled eggs and bacon, to clear out the refrigerator ahead of the trip home. His parents were drinking Bloody Marys and talking about something in the news with one of the Kennedys. Clyde the dog was on the kitchen floor, looking up for bacon bits, which Rex gave him now and then.

"That poor girl," Rex's mom said, "and her poor parents. She was only twenty-eight."

"Kennedy's fault, probably half drunk, driving around the ocean."

"You don't know that! Maybe it was just dark."

Rex's dad shifted around in his chair while he shoveled eggs in his mouth. "Maybe. But he'll never be president."

Rex's mom shook her head and looked a little teary-eyed. "It's just a tragedy what water can do. That's why you boys should never go swimming on a red flag day." She turned to Patrick. "I was so happy to hear you and Rex just played checkers today at your cottage and didn't go swimming."

Rex looked at Patrick and Patrick nodded to Rex's parents.

"So how's your family, after all the excitement today?" Rex's dad asked. He had the stock page of the newspaper on the table next to him, studying while he ate.

"Oh, fine."

"Your dad will probably be glad to get back to the office Monday and relax after this vacation." He kept his head down and circled a stock of interest.

"It's just a miracle everyone's OK," Rex's mom said. "I'm glad to have witnessed it. And it was a miracle that Mr. Jawthorne knew what to do. You never know what secret ways a person has."

"Well, he's from the South. They all know how to deliver horses and puppies down there," Rex's dad said.

"We be excused?" Rex said. "Something to do; won't take long."

"Say goodbye to those girls?" Rex's mom said, smiling at her husband. Rex's dad looked up from the stock page. He shook his head and smirked.

"All right," Rex's mom said, "but don't be gone all night."

"You hear that last part?" Rex's dad said pointing his fork at Rex. "You need to help pack the car." A yellow crumb of scrambled egg rocketed out while he spoke. "You've had fun all week."

"We won't be long." Rex sprang up and ran upstairs to brush his teeth. Then he came down with his hair combed over wet; he was chewing Wrigley's Spearmint gum. He gave Patrick a piece, and they busted out the screen door, running for the Khardomah Lodge.

When they got there, the Cinderella pinball machine was quiet, and there was nobody around. Rex tapped on the countertop bell, and Miss Gert came limping downstairs with a broom.

"Yes?"

"Miss Gert, could you ring up the Jawthorne girls?" Rex said. "They must be upstairs getting ready. We came to say goodbye before their trip."

"Oh, honey, they left hours ago." The man-on-the-moon grandfather clock started chiming loudly.

Rex and Patrick looked at each other. Patrick looked at the clock. The man on the moon was smiling, laughing at them.

"Are you sure?" Rex demanded. "When?"

"Oh, they left during the storm," she said, raising her voice over the chimes. "It was such a rainy, red flag day they couldn't go to the beach, so Mr. Jawthorne cut the trip short."

Rex walked away without saying anything and went over by the pinball machine and sat on a stool.

"Well, thank you, Miss Gert. Thank you for telling us," Patrick said.

She went back upstairs and Patrick went over to Rex. The last chime sounded. Rex was shaking his head. Patrick got out a quarter and put it in the pinball machine. He pulled back the lever and watched the silver ball shoot up the alley, bouncing off lighted bumpers, dinging and racking up points. With the kissing crisis past, Patrick's concentration was better than ever. He executed a back-from-the-dead flipper shot, tipping the edge of the ball with one flipper and then smacking it back up into play with the other. "That's it. Get up there!" He was talking to the ball, and the ball was listening. It obeyed his every wish, and then something he had never seen before happened—the red "extra ball" light was lit. "Rex, look, I got the special lit up!"

Rex unplugged the game, and the ball ran down the gutter.

"Hey!"

"Let's go." Shoulders slumped, Rex started for the door. They left the Khardomah Lodge and walked out into the night. It was cool outside after the rain, and trees were dripping. The wind felt almost like a September evening, when undone homework is remembered just before bed. They walked along feeling spent and ended up in Rex's cottage yard. Both looked up the hill at the cottage across the street where the girl from Indiana stayed. No lights, except the porch. Her family was out.

"Well, maybe I'll see you tomorrow before we leave," Patrick said. "Have to go help pack."

"We still have one last chance," Rex whispered.

"For what?"

"Shhhhh…." He lowered his voice. "I found her dog."

"Wait, what? You found her dog?"

"Found him this morning, before you came over. I tried to tell you, but Mom butted in."

Patrick and Rex were about to have the BIG FIGHT. "You found her dog?"

"Found him this morning, before you came over. I tried to tell you, but Mom butted in."

Deep down, Patrick liked Rex.

"Where is he?"

"Behind our cottage."

Rex had helped Patrick see the world the way it was, all the hidden things.

"Where?"

"By the big tree, where we hid the minibike."

And he helped Patrick make plans and not just let the vacation happen.

"Way back in the woods?"

"He's OK. I got him leashed up safe with some food and water."

But what Rex told him next made Patrick go berserk.

"That's great. Let's go give him back to her."

"Not, now. It has to be the right moment, when she comes out alone, like in the morning. Then I can collect my reward."

"Reward?"

Rex puckered his lips and made a sick, kissing sound. That was it. Patrick dove at him, and they landed with a thud in the sandy yard. Patrick's hands gripped Rex's neck squeezing as hard as he could. Rex was shocked, but he regained his senses and wrestled Patrick around to where he was on the bottom, and Rex was on top choking Patrick. Rex gave Patrick one of his wild-eyed stares, like the time he rode the minibike behind the A&W to rescue him from the bikers.

"What do you want me to do? Just put the dog on her screen porch with nobody home?" He let up choking Patrick to hear his answer.

Patrick gasped for air with his chest heaving. "You can't make her wait. Her dead dad gave her that dog." Patrick grabbed a fistful of sand and threw it in Rex's eyes, just like in the movies. It worked. Rex closed his eyes and Patrick shoved him to the side and was on top of him this time. That's when Rex's mom came out yelling at them both.

"Boys, boys!" she said, pulling them apart. "Stop this! My God, what could be so important?"

She separated them and made them stand up and clean off. Rex's dad came out carrying luggage to the car and yelled for Rex to quit fooling around and help him.

"You boys have had such a nice week together. What's wrong with you two?" Rex's mom said.

"Nothing," Rex said.

"I know what it is, and it's not worth it," she said. "Don't let those Atlanta girls spoil your friendship. Now shake and make up."

Rex stuck out his hand, and Patrick shook it. But their grips were still hard and mean, like an unsettled argument.

"Come on, Rex, bring out your luggage," his dad called. "The fun is over."

Rex walked away, and his mom gave Patrick a curious look, trying to figure out what it was all about. Patrick thought about how she tackled him that first night he slept over, and the way they stole her wig and cut it to shreds for a disguise, and the way she called for the ambulance and watched baby Joey and

Elizabeth when the new baby came. She was a good mom, and Patrick liked her. Patrick took a deep breath to tell Rex's mom the whole story. But he couldn't. He knew from past troubles that things only get worse when parents help.

# - chapter thirty-two -

HALFWAY BACK TO HIS COTTAGE, Patrick decided to rescue the dog. Right now. No delays. Just get the dog and leave it on the girl from Indiana's front porch. No Rex and no reward. All he needed was a flashlight for the woods. He started running. Dad saw him coming from where he was packing the station wagon. "Hey, Patrick, what took so long? You're brothers are doing all the heavy lifting. Look alive."

Patrick tried to look alive, watching Dad rearrange the luggage on top like a puzzle, making all the pieces fit snugly until there was no more room for anything else. Then came the canvas tarp. It seemed just five minutes ago, at the start of the trip, they had cast it aide in the bushes by the cottage. Now they were pulling it out, brushing off leaves and spiders. Dad hurled the tarp over the luggage and told the boys to help put the rope through the brass holes along the edges. Then he tied the tarp onto the luggage rack. To make sure the luggage wouldn't fall off on the highway, he looped two final ropes going lengthwise and two more going across. Navy knots and grunting, sticking the tip of his tongue out to the side, cutting the rope with a pocketknife. Dad was alert and in charge while the boys mostly watched. And the whole time, he talked about how they'd had a good trip and should look forward to going back home and getting back to real life.

"Can I go look on the lookout?" Patrick asked.

"You just got back. Make yourself useful and go change Joey's diaper."

That was the worst. Patrick opened up baby Joey's diaper inside on the rug and saw a smeared explosion of brown death. Gloppy, peanut-butter-like goo was clinging to the goose bumps of baby Joey's bottom while Patrick tried to wipe it clean. The whole time, Joey was laughing and Patrick was whipping his head to the side to avoid the rush of smells that made his throat catch like carnival-ride vomit was ready to come up. Finally, when he got baby Joey clean and Pampered-up fresh, Patrick looked under his fingernails and saw the poo had found a new home. Dashing to the kitchen sink, he lathered up and rinsed again and again, using one fingernail to clean out another, with the poo changing fingernails to start a new colony under a different fingernail and avoid going down the drain. At last, he was ready to get the flashlight and slip away for the dog.

"Patrick, that's good work," Dad said, coming through the kitchen. "I wonder if you could help me carry out my antiques."

So Patrick followed Dad up to his bedroom where he had a shrine of the Civil War pictures he had captured. They were all wrapped in cardboard and plastic, able to survive even if the car went off a cliff and everybody died.

"Be careful, these are one of a kind," he added.

They carried the Civil War items down and out to the car, where Dad slotted them between the middle seat and the way back seat. It would block his view out the rear window, but that's OK, he said. That's what side-view mirrors are for.

The flashlight Patrick needed to go rescue the girl from Indiana's dog was in the kitchen next to the refrigerator in a little cabinet. He had seen it before when looking for birthday candles. So he wandered back in and found it, but the batteries were dead. He remembered down in the basement, they had some odds and ends in a little tool area. Rooting around there, he found a couple of big, fat D batteries still in the wrapper and put them in the flashlight. It worked. All he had to do now was get back outside and sneak off.

But Elizabeth started crying. When Patrick came up from the basement, Dad was comforting her.

"I know, I know you miss your mom," he said. "It's OK. She's with the new baby, with baby Betsy. Where's *your* Betsy Wetsy?"

"Upstairs."

"Well, why don't you go brush your teeth, and Patrick will read a bedtime story to you and Betsy Wetsy."

"Dad? I wanted to go look at the lake."

"No, Patrick, I need you to put Elizabeth to bed." Then he turned to the others. "John, you put Joey to bed. Teddy, you get to bed, too."

"OK," they all said.

Up the stairs Patrick went, holding Elizabeth's hand, with the flashlight hidden in his pocket. She took forever brushing her teeth. No quick once around the molars and spitting like a boy. Girls brushed their teeth in slow motion, the same way moms went shopping for clothes. Then he lay in bed with Elizabeth and Betsy Wetsy. He could see why she felt sad. Her dark-paneled room was small and gloomy to face at night without Mom. Mom always tucked her in, kissed her, and read her some books. The only book not packed and still on the bed stand was *Go Dog Go.*

Patrick read her the story, which was page after page of hypnotic sentences designed to make kids sleepy. "Do you like my hat?" he read while the whole time he kept thinking about the girl from Indiana's dog out there in the woods, tied up to a tree in the dark with a leash. He had to wrap things up and get going.

"Goodnight, Elizabeth," he said, covering her up to leave.

"Aren't you going to pray?"

"No, not tonight."

"Mom does."

"Well, you pray for her."

Elizabeth closed her eyes and folded her hands. Her lips were moving, but Patrick couldn't hear the words. The only thing he caught was at the very end. "And please, God, no monsters tonight. Amen."

Now, finally, Patrick hurried downstairs to bust out, but Dad was right there, sitting in the living room watching *The Tonight Show* with Johnny Carson. Dad was laughing at some joke but noticed Patrick easing down the steps.

"Patrick, what are you doing up? We've got a big day tomorrow."

"I just wanted to take one more look at the lake from the lookout."

"No way, you've had enough running around this trip. Get some rest. We'll all say goodbye to the lake in the morning."

Johnny Carson said something funny to Ed McMahon, and the audience laughed. Dad and Patrick looked at the TV to see what it was. Patrick was hoping Dad would get caught up in the show and he could slide out the door. But then a singer came on who was boring. Dad looked back at him. "OK,

Patrick, get to bed."

"Goodnight, Dad."

"Goodnight, Patrick. You're a good man. You'll do all right."

Patrick dragged upstairs with the flashlight in his pocket, feeling trapped. The only thing to do was pretend to go to bed and listen for when Dad came upstairs so he could sneak out later. He got in bed with his clothes and shoes on and put the flashlight under his pillow. The window was half open and there was a lake breeze. He could hear the waves landing and Johnny Carson talking and Dad laughing now and then. Patrick had to slap his face to stay awake, and take a deep breath and widen his eyes to stay serious. Fidgeting around he found something in his shirt pocket and pulled it out. It was a piece of paper. He turned on the flashlight and saw it was the article on the Mothman.

# - chapter thirty-three -

WHEN PATRICK WOKE UP, the cottage was dark. Not a sound. He listened for the TV downstairs and heard only the foghorn out on the pier. It was a low, deep note that stretched over the water then stopped cold with a stabbing echo inland. He looked at his watch: three forty-five. His legs slid from under the covers, and his Keds touched the floor.

Opening his bedroom door, Patrick could hear Dad snoring and everybody else breathing deeply. After stuffing the flashlight in his pocket, he tiptoed downstairs. This was a time of night he had never seen before at the cottage. The living room chairs looked haunted, as if all the dead people who once vacationed there were watching him. Ghosts in straw hats and bonnets and flapper girl swimsuits spied him moving toward the kitchen. They didn't say anything. Their eyes followed his hand reaching for the doorknob. He turned it as quietly as a safe cracker, and he was free.

Right away, the lake air and the surf lapping and the bug music cheered him up a little. He looked around. Nobody. Every cottage was dark. The stars were out. The moon was shaped like a toenail clipping without much light. Patrick wondered what the astronauts were doing—probably playing twenty questions with the moon still up ahead. The family station wagon with the tight ropes on the luggage rack was as sad as a funeral hearse ready for morning. Patrick sneaked down the road with the sand pebbles and asphalt whispering underfoot like Rice Krispies and milk.

This was the perfect time for a smoke. He could go for one of those cigars

Mr. Jawthorne used, or a Camel or Winston, the kind his friends passed around back by the train tracks at home. His fingers made a mechanical reach for his shirt pocket for a cigarette and instead found the article on Mothman. He didn't even pull it out. He recognized the feel of it and took his fingers back fast.

Up ahead a porch light shined at the girl from Indiana's yellow cottage. At the bottom of the steps, her mom's blue Saab was packed and ready to leave. All the renters had to leave on Saturday in Grand Haven. He stopped and thought maybe his whole mission was a mistake. What if Rex had already dropped off the dog earlier and he didn't know? He sneaked up the stone steps to her cottage yard and spied around. There were two dog bowls there. He leaned closer. One was full of water, and the other was full of dog food, so he knew her dog was still missing. He headed back down the steps and over toward the woods behind Rex's cottage to rescue Sandy.

When he got to Rex's place, he stopped to think. Their Country Squire was packed on top, too, and nobody was stirring. But all the bedroom windows were open, and Patrick remembered Rex's dog, Clyde. If Clyde barked, Rex would come out and ruin the rescue. So he flanked around the yard and approached the woods from a path a little out of the way and left the flashlight off.

The sandy path led him down a steep hill with towering pine trees and little ivy bushes and weed trees twisting up chest high. It got darker and damper with each step. Sand shifted under his Keds, pine needles dripped raindrops, clammy weed branches dragged across his arms, and then a spider web stretched across his face. He slapped it fast to kill any spider about to bite and decided it was time to get out the flashlight.

He flicked the button. But there was no light. Again, he flicked the switch on and off. Nothing.

Damn.

He wound up the flashlight and slapped it on his palm and it came on, but the light was weak because the batteries had been old when he unwrapped them. He had to work fast to find the big tree where Rex said the dog was tied up. This took him off the path, cracking through fallen branches and a thicket of prickly overgrowth on the backside of Rex's place. He used the flashlight to watch for danger, aiming on the ground and then up about eye level in the trees. He didn't want to run into a skunk. That's when he saw it.

Red eyes. Looking right at him about twenty feet ahead. He remembered what the article said about Mothman—how his eyes glowed as red as bicycle reflectors.

He stopped. His heart pumped full blast. The eyes staring at him were as red as bicycle reflectors. He blinked. They *were* bicycle reflectors. It was a pair of rusty bikes somebody had heaped atop each other, now overtaken by vines.

"There's no Mothman," he said to himself.

He took a deep breath and kept going, ashamed that he had thought it was the Mothman. After some loud trouncing through the brush, he saw the trunk of the big tree up ahead where he and Rex had hid the minibike. That's where Sandy would be. Just get him and get out of these woods. This was it. He ran for it and pointed the light all around. There was the water bowl and the empty dog food bowl. Yes. And there was the leash, or the end of it, around the other side of the tree. He scooted around the trunk, training his flashlight forward.

"Here, Sandy? Sandy?" he whispered.

The flashlight beam followed the line of the leash to the very end. What? The leash was broken, with wet chew marks on the end. The dog was gone.

SHIT. He called out for the dog in a whisper and then whistled a little.

Nothing.

He pointed the flashlight all around in a circle and saw nothing but woods, until the battery burned out like a spent match and he was alone in the darkest night. Patrick stood still and turned up his senses. His eyes adjusted to the tree shapes and shadows. His ears noticed the bugs chanting. No breeze. No smell, except maybe a forgotten campfire. That's when he saw the orange flickers on the trees way up ahead. It looked like the reflection of a fire somewhere off in the cemetery. He held his breath and listened and could hear faint voices talking and laughing the way adults do when they drink. And then from the same direction, he heard something he wished he hadn't—a little, tiny *yarf* of a dog bark. Maybe Sandy had broken free and run off toward the sound of human voices in the cemetery. He decided to call it quits.

# - chapter thirty-four -

HE DECIDED TO GO BACK to the cottage and go to bed. Get back under the cool sheets and sleep. But he remembered what happened on the pier during the storm, when he had run to the boat tie and grabbed it tight and waited for the water to hit. At the time, he had done it so he could kiss Ginny. The wave slammed into him like the lake knew his name and hated him. The lake wanted to undo all his finger knots, unwrap his arms, and swallow him up. Then it pulled back out with one more tug, tempting him with sweet whispers to please come along. *I promise*, the lake said, *just let go. Let go, and you won't have to watch your dad die. LET GO RIGHT NOW!* His arms had loosened. His mind was giving in. His fingers were slipping. But before it took him, the foam fell away from him in a billion bubbles. Cheers broke out. He gulped a breath and got up on shaky legs to run back to the fog house. The football players backslapped him with curse words of respect. Rex, John, and Teddy hugged him. He had made it. They retreated from the end of the pier in a hurry—and Patrick had run the fastest—because he knew what the lake wanted. It wanted *him*. Now, when he saw the campfire in the cemetery, he didn't want to go there either. But he thought of surviving the boat tie and took a few steps forward.

Footsteps snapped brush right behind him.

He turned around. It was Rex.

"SHHHHHHH …" he said.

"What are you doing?" Patrick said.

"What are *you* doing?"

"Going after that dog."

"Where is he?"

"Heard a bark, over there."

Rex looked toward the cemetery squinting.

"What'd you care?" Patrick said. "You here to fight?"

Rex looked at the ground, ashamed, and then back at Patrick. "No, I'm here to help."

"Horseshit."

Rex blanched. Patrick had never talked to him like a dad before. "Patrick, really. I couldn't sleep. I should've given him back before. Heard somebody out here and knew it was you."

Patrick thought about it. "If you're lying, I'll beat the shit out of you."

"You couldn't beat the shit of anybody."

Patrick tackled him to the ground, but this time Rex didn't fight back.

"Be cool, man. I'm not lying," Rex said, looking up at Patrick.

"Promise?"

"Promise."

"We get the dog, and *no* reward. Just drop him off and leave."

"OK," Rex said. Patrick got up and helped pull Rex up. Rex stuck out his hand to shake on it. His grip seemed sincere, not like before, so they were back in business. They laughed, and Rex fake-boxed Patrick to show he could have beat the shit out of him if they *had* fought. Patrick was glad to have him along and felt much better about the project. They tiptoed ahead, getting closer to the cemetery. It was about a five-minute slow walk to avoid making noise, the whole time dealing with mosquitos buzzing by their ears and sticky spider webs draped from branches. They could see the steam of their breath, and their faces got sweaty and itchy. Then they soldiered up alongside two opposite trees, hiding behind them and studying the campfire. The encampment was two hundred feet away. They could see the girl from Indiana's dog. It was Sandy, all right. And there were five or six people and motorcycles. Sitting on a log by the fire was the Mothman.

"Let's forget it," Rex said.

# - chapter thirty-five -

WHEN HE FIRST APPEARED in Point Pleasant, West Virginia, in November 1966, the Mothman stood in the road at night as a car with two couples came over a hill by an old TNT plant. They were young people in search of seclusion. There he was. Suddenly in the headlights, a hairy man-like thing with wings on his back. Patrick had read the article Rex gave him about ten times. Seven feet tall, gray in color, red eyes. Waiting. The car tires spun like crazy shooting dust. They raced toward town doing a hundred miles an hour. When they looked out the rear window, there he was in the sky, a dark-shaped body, his wings fully extended. The Mothman was going as fast as the car. The driver went faster. Pulling into a farm they felt they were finally safe, and AGAIN, there he was in the headlights, waiting for them. The Mothman was standing in the middle of the dirt road with a dead dog at his side. Rex said he probably killed the dog for a snack before he could eat some humans, but that part was a little unclear. The driver raced away like Steve McQueen in *Bullitt* and came back with police. They never did find the dog. In the coming months, the Mothman chased lots of other townspeople, too, Rex had said, but they all got away. About a year later, the Silver Bridge collapsed into the Ohio River during rush hour, and forty-six people died. Two of the bodies were never found.

Patrick and Rex leaned against their separate trees watching and thinking. They could see the Mothman holding the dog, petting it, and some of the others were sitting around drinking and smoking. The campfire light danced on the tombstones and the chrome of the parked motorcycles. The boys waited about a half hour, hugging trees, not saying a word. Patrick leaned his face against the bark and closed his eyes.

In July 1953, Bobby Mauthmunn was eight years old when he first came to Grand Haven for a week's vacation. He was with his mother and her parents on a trip to cheer up. It was the month Bobby's dad had run out on the family. He left without saying goodbye to Bobby or explaining why he was leaving. Up until then, it had been a good summer for the shy boy who collected Buffalo nickels and played in the creek, looking for turtles. It had also been the summer Bobby's mother sent him to Vacation Bible School to escape the heat on June nights. The sermon one night was about Lazarus, and Bobby had raised his hand when the pastor looked at him and asked if anybody wanted to trust Jesus. Other children were raising their hands, so why not? They gave Bobby a pocket New Testament, which he read on walks in the woods, pretending he was Lazarus back from the dead. He took to saving turtles caught in traffic ,trying to cross the road. Jesus had saved him, and now he was saving turtles. He would sit on a tree stump and run to pick them up and carry them to safety across the road by the creek.

Then his dad left. He took it hard. In bed at night, he prayed for him to come back. He even prayed in Grand Haven in 1953 on the pier walking alone. But his dad never came back.

Middle school, high school, cutting school—there was still no sign of his dad. Smoking, beer parties, girlfriends, marijuana, a motorcycle, dropping out, speeding tickets, missed court dates, drunken nights, campfire fights, a warrant for his arrest, a burglary at a hardware store, caught by police, county jail time, leg shackles, state court, and a choice: state prison or the Army. "Sometimes the military can provide the structure a young man needs," the judge advised. So off went Bobby to boot camp where he got a buzz cut, did sit-ups, and took target practice. Then came the letter from his mom: "P.S. I think you should know, your father died."

Then Bobby went to Vietnam.

Vietnam was a place in the jungle on the edge of death. Other GIs hated it, but not Bobby Mauthmunn. He liked it. It was structure. He became a man of the jungle, rising from the mud, charging at the enemy, taking chances, and dispensing destruction to clear his mind. More cautious soldiers placed bets on how long "Mothman" would last. But he never got shot and always stabbed first. Bobby racked up kills like a ball of rubber bands, adding one at a time as the ball got bigger and bigger. A visiting commander remarked that Bobby Mauthmunn was exemplary, an instrument of U.S. foreign policy thwarting communist aggression in Southeast Asia. Yes, sir, thank you, sir. What was his secret? No one knew. He didn't know, didn't care. Killing was something to do, and he did it mechanically. Fight, kill, eat, sleep, march, fight, kill.... Then, suddenly, his year was almost up. Everyone told him go home, go back to the world. Get out, Mothman, before you get killed. He planned to re-enlist, because there was nothing for him back home. But then he saw the turtle. It was up ahead, crossing a dirt road, and he stopped to watch it. He remembered the boy he once was and didn't like the reminder. He hoisted his M-16. BLAM. Turtle guts, turtle shell shards, and turtle blood splattered the road. Marching on for miles, he was bothered more by that dead turtle than all the people he had killed. He decided to go back to Illinois and try the hundred-day plan.

Chopper ride, plane ride, car ride, civilian clothes, no rules, welcome home. It wasn't easy. There was no more structure. Bar fights, punching his stepfather by the refrigerator, getting slapped by his mom, feeling like stabbing them both and watching their blood run on the kitchen linoleum, and then maybe burning the house down like a village hut. What was wrong with him? It was Day 90. He had hoped to be getting better by now. To avoid bloodshed, he turned to his motorcycle on a hot July night and joined a few old friends to go on a road trip and see what Day 100 might look like.

On the trip he had pulled into Grand Haven for the first time since he had been there in 1953, faintly recognizing the place. That was the day they went to A&W, the day he was tempted to kill the boy who had thrown the Wonder Bread bag that stuck to his tailpipe. Now he was on Day 99. One more day, and then what? Would he be cured? Or would it always feel like this? He sat by the fire, petting the dog that had wandered into camp. The others had gone to bed down. With each stroke of his hand on Sandy's back, he remembered a face of someone he had killed. They died again for him like a movie trailer, one after another. He was on acid. The dog was blood red. The dog was white. The dog was his mother, telling him to come home. The campfire flickered. The dog was just a dog again. Maybe if he killed the dog, he could get it all out of his system. Maybe not. Maybe he should cut the throats of his friends as they slept, or kill the first person that moved, just as a game. He could almost taste killing in his mouth, the way a former smoker holds that first cigarette, ready to light up after a failed attempt to quit. He stopped petting the dog to listen to something he thought he heard behind him on the edge of the woods.

"Psssssst," Rex whispered.

Patrick jolted awake and looked. The other bikers had lain down on sleeping bags, and the Mothman was alone on a log with the dog on his lap and his back to them.

"Wait here," Patrick whispered.

With the same resolve he had mustered on the pier when he decided to go for the boat tie between waves, he walked toward the dog. The cemetery grass was wet and quiet. Tombstones rippled past him. He moved in a straight line toward the Mothman. Patrick didn't believe in the Mothman the way Rex did, but he had hung around Rex's strange beliefs long enough to catch them like a cold. Patrick's fears shifted back and forth from facing the Mothman who was a biker to facing the Mothman who had killed those people in West Virginia. Neither one was any good. What would Patrick do? He didn't know. Maybe grab the dog and run. Maybe grab a burning stick from the campfire and stab the Mothman in the eye and then grab the dog. Maybe push him in the fire, and then grab the dog. His heart was pounding worse than when he was going to the principal's office, even worse than the time he was arrested for robbing the Ben Franklin. He was so afraid, he stopped to say a prayer. But his tongue had run out of spit, and he had no worthy prayers on the shelf. All he could think of was the prayer he had heard Elizabeth say earlier that night. "And please, God, no monsters tonight. Amen."

Bobby Mauthmann could hear the footsteps and touched the handle of his knife on his belt holster.

Patrick walked slowly into view on the far side of the fire and stood where they could see each other through the smoke. The Mothman said nothing. He looked at Patrick's hands. Empty. He looked at Patrick's face. Afraid. The Mothman's eyes were listening and ready. The dog saw Patrick and wriggled a little while the Mothman held him tight and kept slowly petting him.

"I came for the dog."

Right away some of the others heard Patrick and got up. They rose from their sleeping bags in the shadows like phantoms rising from their graves. They were all still high or drunk and capable of crimes they might do in a dream but would never do in the sunlight. The big redheaded one, the Viking, came over to the fire, rubbing his eyes, looking around to see if anybody else was coming out of the night. "What the hell are you doing out this hour?" he demanded. He got close enough for Patrick to smell his B.O. and whiskey dribbles on his red beard.

"The dog," Patrick said, his voice cracking. "I came for the dog."

Others walked around him, looking at his face, poking him. There were two other men and two women. One was the woman with the long braided hair down her back. She was the former state highway worker who had quit her job holding the SLOW sign, which was a mean, hot, suffering job that made her hate the tourists always going someplace better.

"That dog belongs to us," she said, standing on her barefoot tiptoes. "Be damned if we don't take him with us."

Patrick tried to keep his head down, so they wouldn't remember him. "I'm sorry, but that dog belongs to a girl whose dad gave it to her before he died. She misses her dad, and she's very sad for her dog, and—"

"Boo-hoo…." They all started fake-crying and then laughing at Patrick. All of them except the Mothman. He kept quiet and watched.

"Hey," the SLOW sign woman said. "It's *the kid.* The Wonder Bread bag kid."

They all stopped laughing and moved in closer to see for themselves in the campfire light. Sure enough, it was him. They got close enough for Patrick to hear their soft grunting and smell their cigarette hair and smoky campfire clothes.

"Shit, it *is* him!" the Viking one said, shoving Patrick's shoulder. "He got away last time, but this time—"

Suddenly, Rex came yelping at a gallop with an oak tree branch in his hands. He had grabbed it for style and was charging out of the darkness like an Indian chief. The other woman, the frizzy-haired one who had skipped out on her job as a waitress for the trip, with no definite plans for the future, bumped him from the side with a hockey check, and he fell on his face. Now they had two boys by the shirts, held together for inspection in the glow of the fire.

"Kill me, but let him go with the dog!" Rex said, starting to cry. "It's all my fault."

"You're a brave and honest boy to say so," the waitress woman said. She hated kids because they always left a sloppy milk mess and french fries on the floor for her to clean up, and their parents never had decent money for the tip.

"Thanks," Rex said, feeling encouraged.

She smiled and punched him in the stomach as hard as she could. Rex doubled up, coughing out spit and cuss words to himself.

"I say we throw them in the hole," another one said.

They all laughed and seemed to agree, except the Mothman. He just petted the dog and said nothing. The Viking led them past some tombstones to a yellow construction backhoe, parked in front of an open grave. The freshly dug grave was six feet deep and flooded with a half foot of rainwater from the thunderstorm. He pushed them in, and they landed with a splash. The bottom of the grave was squishy and soft like the modeling clay John had made into Jesus and John Lennon and the naked woman. Patrick and Rex stood up right away, dripping with water that smelled of urine from the men relieving themselves earlier. The gang gathered around the sides of the grave and looked down on them. Patrick and Rex grabbed tree roots on the side, pulling themselves back up above ground. When they got to the top they were covered with mud, and the gang pushed them in again. SPLASH. Cold, muddy water ran down their faces, into their eyes and mouths, as they climbed out again and got pushed in once more to a roar of laughter from the bikers. After three times, they made it to the top exhausted.

"Have they learned their lesson, or should we cut them?" the waitress woman said. She was only bluffing to scare them, but as she said the words, they sounded good and right. The others took the words in and and fixed their eyes on the boys.

Nobody answered. And that was the longest wait. Not a sound, except for a symphony of bugs suffering through night in the woods. Patrick watched the bikers' hands to see who would show a knife. The boys could have both yelled for help as loud as they wanted, but only the dead would've heard them, and the dead probably wanted them dead. Patrick and Rex sat up, looking for some gap in the legs to run. But they were walled in all around them.

The Viking licked his lips and got out a small pocketknife and stepped toward Patrick, holding it out front so all could see. It was only a two-inch-long knife he used on tree-trimming jobs to cut fruit slices on his lunch break. He was drunk and secretly wished he had been to Vietnam and back. Never before had he killed anybody, but he wanted to show the others—and himself—that he was bad enough, even if he just cut one of them a little.

Besides, the other night outside the movie theatre when that crazy man with the gun humiliated them, the Mothman didn't do anything. Mothman just held back, avoiding a fight. Mothman was slipping. The gang all wondered why he didn't go all jungle and snap the man's neck. This was the Viking's chance to ascend to prominence and do something solid. "I don't think they've learned their lesson yet," he said walking toward them.

Over by the campfire, the Mothman got up. He hadn't moved the whole time. He was taller than the rest of them, and the boys saw him coming.

"Please, let us go," Rex said. "You can keep the dog."

The Mothman walked through the crowd, holding the dog. He stood between the biker with the knife and the boys. He got out his own knife, a hunting knife with a six-inch blade. Everyone watched.

"Get up," the Mothman told the boys.

They got up. He looked at their faces and didn't say anything. His eyes vacuumed the thoughts out of Patrick and Rex to learn everything he could about them without giving any hint of what he might do next. It was Day 99 still, and not yet light.

"Mothman's been to Vietnam," the SLOW sign woman told the boys, pointing at them with a trembling finger. "He killed a lot of people over there, and he don't deserve to have you throwing piss at him in his own country on the highway. You little shits. You worthless, tourist pieces of shit. You showed him disrespect, and now he's gonna kill you. Get ready to DIE." Her eyes bulged, and she looked at the Mothman with all the strength she had to usher in the killings. The gang could feel it. There was going to be blood on the grass and two dead boys in the cemetery, and the bikers would leave before sunup, with no one knowing who did it or why.

Patrick and Rex looked at the Mothman. A breeze blew through the cemetery that cooled the mud on their faces and arms. Bobby Mauthmunn took a deep breath, as if to send oxygen to his knife-wielding hand. But he looked at the open grave and the muddy boys and lowered his knife. Something from his boyhood came out of his mouth, almost like a prayer, which he wasn't even sure was possible.

"Lazarus, come forth."

Rex and Patrick looked at each other. They had no idea what that meant, but it seemed to be something good. Bobby Mauthmunn handed Patrick the dog. The boys gulped and ran off into the woods.

# - chapter thirty-six -

SUNRISE WAS CLOSE. The stars were out, but gray streaks of tomorrow were pushing away the night from behind the trees. The wind had shifted from the south and left the lake warm and easy. They took turns holding the dog while the other one dove into the surf to get the mud off. Then they took Sandy swimming to wash the cemetery off him, too. The boys shampooed their hair with sand and rubbed the water on every spot where the grave had shamed them. They were still shaky and in shock from what had happened. Walking back through the woods, Rex had talked the whole time about his theories on the Mothman and why he didn't kill them or at least eat the dog. Now, the water seemed to bring him to his closing argument.

"Maybe the Mothman was trying to *save* those people in West Virginia from the bridge," Rex said, "the way he saved us. What do you think?"

"Rex."

"Yeah?"

"There's no such thing as Mothman." Patrick handed Rex the water-soaked newspaper article from his shirt pocket, which Rex handled with archival care, putting it in his own pocket for safekeeping.

Patrick picked up the dog under his arm, and they left the shore. By the road, they turned around and looked at the empty beach and the fishing boats motoring out past the lighthouse. It was the dawn of another summer day in Grand Haven but a day they both would miss.

"I hear the winter here, they have ice from the shore to pier," Rex said.

They walked up the wooden steps to the lookout, and then across the curving road to the girl from Indiana's cottage. Up her stone steps they went in their wet shoes. Water squirted out the side air holes of Patrick's Keds. "Better let me," Rex said, taking the dog from Patrick as the cottage got closer with each step. Not talking, not even a whisper, they reached the top and looked around. The screen porch door was shut. Her cottage was dark. That's when the dog wanted free. He recognized the spot where the girl from Indiana would let him out every morning and gather him up to kiss him. Rex set him down awkwardly, half dropping him, and Sandy let out a *yarf.* Then he ran up the steps, scratching on the screen door and barking even louder. Patrick looked at Rex.

"We should go now," Patrick said.

"Yeah."

This was it. All they had to do was run off, and she would never know. But they couldn't. They wanted to see her once more without binoculars. A light came on upstairs. Then thundering footsteps, the door flying open, and out came the girl from Indiana like an angel in a white night shirt with her blonde hair riding over shoulder.

"Sandy!" she yelled, scooping him up and kissing him. "You're all wet." She looked at Patrick and didn't recognize him, then looked at Rex. She seemed to remember him.

"*You* ... did you find him in the lake?"

"Yeah, we rescued him from drowning."

Patrick looked at Rex. He couldn't believe Rex was making up a lie. Rex always knew what to say.

"What happened?" she asked, holding the dog to her cheek.

"Well, we got up early for one last jog around and a look at the lake. We like to exercise." Rex patted his stomach muscles and did a Jack Lalanne knee squat. Then he came back up and continued. "Anyway, we thought we heard a dog struggling in the water ..." Rex described how they had run in the water and swam out to get him.

"You did *all that* to save him?"

Rex shrugged. "It wasn't me. Patrick, here, he swam the farthest, way out past the danger buoy. I was ready to give up. I said, 'Think of your own life, not some dog.' But he said, 'No, we have to save that dog. That dog must mean something to somebody.'"

"Patrick? Is that your name?" She turned to him.

"Yeah."

"You risked *your own* life?"

"Well—"

She put down the dog and grabbed his face between the open palms of her hands and kissed him on the lips. It was different than any kiss he had ever had before from his mom. The girl from Indiana had bad breath from just waking up, but he didn't mind. Her lips were telling the story of how much she loved her dad, and how she still missed him every day, and how nobody understood her, and how her life had collapsed like an old barn when she lost that dog, and now, how back-from-the-dead she felt, having him home safe again. Patrick's lips were the target of all those feelings and other ones she threw in extra. Her lips told him she didn't really like the boys she had gone to the movie theatre with and wished she wasn't in high school and wished she were young again like Patrick and Rex. She was jealous of their youth, the way they were jealous of her being older. Then she turned to Rex and did the same to him. The screen door opened. It was her mother, in a blue plaid bathrobe.

"Sandy? Is that you?"

The dog ran up to greet the mother, and the three of them—mother, daughter, and dog—hugged and cried. Patrick and Rex looked at each other and nodded. It was time to go. They eased backwards toward the steps.

"Wait!" the mom said. "The reward!"

"No, we can't take any reward," Rex said.

"But my purse is right inside; wait."

"No, we have to go," Rex said. "You can buy us an ice cream next summer at Dairy Treat."

"Next summer? Who of us knows whether we'll live to see another summer?" the mom said.

The boys turned and walked down the stone steps.

"Thanks," the girl from Indiana called out.

Patrick and Rex got to the bottom and turned out of view. Rex leaned against a retaining wall, feeling his lips with his fingertips. "How many weeks until next summer?" he moaned. "*Was that not incredible?* Could you believe that?"

"I gotta go before my parents wake up."

"OK."

They shook hands, and then Rex did something unbelievable. He reached for his wallet and gave Patrick a five-dollar bill. Patrick looked at Lincoln's face and then up at Rex's.

"Rex, you don't have to—"
"No, you were *first*, but really, we both won."
"We did."
"We made it to the moon."

# - chapter thirty-seven -

NOBODY HEARD PATRICK sneak back in. The cottage was quiet. He stripped naked, put on dry underwear and climbed back in bed at six thirty, falling fast asleep. When it was time to get up, he was too sore to move. His head hurt, and his arms and legs were tired. He had scratch marks and itches and no energy.

"Patrick, we have to go," Dad said, jostling his shoulder. "Everyone else is downstairs eating cereal."

He dragged out of bed and went into the bathroom to splash some water in his face. Looking over, he saw the canister of itchy bottom powder and decided to put some on his back to see if it was any good. For breakfast he had Cap'n Crunch and orange juice and sat on the deck to watch the lake. The lake was blue, and the lighthouse was catsup red in the sun. White sailboats leaned into the horizon. He saw joggers, kite flyers, dog walkers, and the early sunbathers spreading out their towels. Teddy, Elizabeth, and baby Joey were watching a Bugs Bunny cartoon inside. But John came out to be with Patrick and look at the lake.

"It shouldn't be this way," John said.

"What?"

"The vacation shouldn't end. It should last forever."

"Yeah."

"When I grow up and my band takes off, I'm going to buy one of these cottages and live here year-round. You can come, too."

"Rex says in the winter time they have ice from shore to pier."

"Leave it to Rex. I never thought about that."

"Me neither."

"I guess I thought in Grand Haven, it's always a summer day."

Dad hollered for them. "All right, everybody, let's go." He unplugged the rental TV and carried it out to the car to return. The boys washed their dishes and put them away for the next people. Dad made them take out the trash, wipe off the table with a wet rag, sweep once more, pick up pieces from the game Battleship, and check under the couch for chicken bones so they wouldn't lose their rental deposit.

"Is everybody ready?" Dad said.

Dad carried baby Joey out to the car and strapped him in. John and Teddy and Elizabeth went outside. Patrick opened the freezer to look for a Popsicle or something good. But the only thing left was ice cubes and the stringer of fish from the first day. The dead fish eyes looked at Patrick, blank but knowing. They knew that someday Patrick would be dead, too. He shut the freezer door and ran out to the car.

Betsy was dressed in pink when they arrived in the hospital room to rescue Mom. She hugged the whole family, and the nurse took a group picture with Mom's Kodak Instamatic camera. Everyone crowded on the hospital bed with Mom and Betsy. The first time the flashcube didn't work, so the nurse took a second picture, and that time it flashed.

"Patrick, why are your shoes all wet?" Mom asked.

"I don't know."

She didn't believe that, but with the new baby, nobody pressed it.

The ride home from vacation was always worse than the ride to vacation. Patrick tried to sleep. The way back seat was windy and hot with all the windows open—and crowded, too, now that Teddy was back there. When Patrick woke up it was around lunchtime, and they pulled into a place called Crown Point, Indiana. Patrick had never heard of it before, but Dad said it was history.

"You mean Civil War?" Patrick asked, getting out of the car at a Burger Chef.

"No, Dillinger."

"Dillinger?"

Dad told Patrick that Dillinger was a famous gangster back in the Depression. He robbed banks but never robbed from the farmers or poor people in the banks. He was Public Enemy Number One. The family sat down and had some Big Chefs and malts in the air conditioning while Dad told the boys how the police finally caught Dillinger and locked him up in the jail at Crown Point. But before they could send him to trial for the electric chair, Dillinger escaped by pointing a fake gun at the guards. Patrick felt proud of him that he had done such good things with his life and fooled the police. Dillinger went to Chicago to have plastic surgery on his face to make him look different. He was free and on vacation for a while, because nobody recognized him. But then a lady in red told the police about him, and they shot Dillinger dead outside a movie theatre. Even Dillinger's vacation came to an end. After lunch, Dad drove everyone past the jail where Dillinger had escaped so the boys could appreciate history, at least from the windows.

"Honey, look at the time," Mom said. "We have to get the new baby home."

"OK, I guess you're right," Dad said.

"And honey, can we *please* turn on the air conditioner for the trip home?"

"Well, OK, I don't like to take chances with the engine, but we'll do it for you and the baby."

"Thanks."

Elizabeth leaned forward.

"Mom?"

"Yes, dear?"

"Where's Teddy?"

An old man reading the paper on his front porch heard the screeching sound and looked up at the station wagon full of kids with luggage on top. Dad hit the brakes and did a U-turn. He raced back to the Burger Chef where Teddy was waiting in the parking lot, sipping his malt through a straw.

"You did it again, guys!" he said, slamming the door after getting in.

"We have got to *wake up* as a family!" Dad said.

"I know. I know," Mom said.

Dad made everyone count off before leaving Crown Point to get back on the highway.

"One," John said,

"Two," Patrick said.

"Three," Teddy said.

"Four," Elizabeth said. Mom counted off five and six for Joey and baby

Betsy. They got on the highway and headed south into the heat. The family station wagon arrived safely back in the driveway at home at nine thirty that night. The next night Walter Cronkite reported that the astronauts landed safely on the moon. Then on Monday, Dad put on his dark suit and tie, grabbed his briefcase, and went downtown. The day after Labor Day, John, Patrick, and Teddy went back to school while Mom stayed home to take care of Elizabeth, Joey, and baby Betsy. Sometimes, on winter nights, they looked at Kodak pictures of the trip and talked about Grand Haven, and Patrick thought about how Rex had taught him all about home runs and how hard they'd tried to kiss Tammy and Ginny but how he was secretly glad they'd left for Atlanta before they could say goodbye. He thought about the biker who'd been to Vietnam, the little lost dog, and the girl from Indiana whose father had died. And he thought about how her lips felt against his and how every kiss should be like that—like a thank you, from one person to another.

# Acknowledgments

With appreciation to the kind townsfolk of Grand Haven, who endure hard winters in solitude, only to arrive at beautiful summers invaded by carloads of tourists. How lovely is the place you call home. Thanks for sharing it with strangers during the best days of the year.

# About the Author

Kevin Killeen's favorite time of the year is the July week spent at a rental cottage in Grand Haven, Michigan—the same town where his parents used to take their large family on summer trips in the 1960s and '70s. When he's not on vacation, Kevin pretends to work as a reporter for KMOX Radio in St. Louis, covering crime, politics, and odd happenings of no consequence. His hobbies include tripping over his children's shoes, turning down loud music, and rubbing his wife's feet while she lies on the living room couch discussing the bills as he stares at the cracks in the ceiling. His first novel, *Never Hug a Nun* (Blank Slate Press, 2012), features the earlier exploits of Patrick Cantwell, set in Webster Groves, Missouri. It won a Ben Franklin award in the humor category from the Independent Book Publishers Association of America.

CPSIA information can be obtained at www.ICGtesting.com
Printed in the USA
LVOW08s0415240614

391360LV00004B/5/P